FACING DEMONS

ASHLEY SANDERS

FACING DEMONS

Order this book online at www.trafford.com
or email orders@trafford.com

Most Trafford titles are also available at major online book retailers.

This is a work of fiction. Characters, locations and events mentioned in
this novel are either a product of the author's imagination or, if real, used
fictitiously without any intent to describe actual conduct.

Cover image provided by Benjamin Dowie

Printed in the United States of America.

ISBN: 978-1-4269-4801-5 (sc)
ISBN: 978-1-4269-5170-1 (hc)

Library of Congress Control Number: 2010918391

Trafford rev. 10/06/2011

 www.trafford.com

North America & international
toll-free: 1 888 232 4444 (USA & Canada)
phone: 250 383 6864 ♦ fax: 812 355 4082

For those who deserve a second chance

If we had no winter,
the spring would not be so pleasant;
if we did not sometimes taste of
adversity, prosperity would not be so welcome.

— Anne Bradstreet

Prologue

Blake Solomon stands frozen in shock in the emergency room, his eyes wide as he watches doctors and nurses attempt to resuscitate the lifeless body.

"How did it come to this?" His voice trembles.

One of the doctors rushes over to Blake.

"Sir, we've been doing surgery for a few hours now but his pulse is fading. We believe that any further attempts at resuscitation will be unsuccessful, what would you like us to do?"

Blake stares blankly at the doctor and then at the motionless boy lying on the gurney. He had done everything in his power to save him, this kid.

He remembers being in this hospital not too long ago, but for a very different reason...

* * * *

Five senior doctors stand at the end of the gentleman's bed pondering the outcome of his treatment.

"It's a miracle."

The patient lay asleep, recovering from what many would describe as being dragged through hell and back again. Several months of chemotherapy to combat one of the most aggressive metastatic cancers these experienced physicians had ever seen and this patient had come out at the end of it without even a trace of being unwell. Certainly, there were months of explosive vomiting and diarrhoea, and the constant prayer that death would come and take away his pain. But this strong man had already been through too much to give up now. He had to make the choice—to fight this battle and live, or allow himself to be consumed by the evil cells destroying his body.

He remembers the good days, being wheeled outside for some fresh air by his son or wife or a kind nurse. He would get a glimmer of willpower and hope instilled inside of him again, forgetting the darkness for but a moment. It was these precious days that kept him pushing through the pain, and helped him forget the bad days where he would lay on the ground next to the toilet bowl, the cool surface easing his fever, whilst awaiting the next stomach explosion. Often he would pass out and just for a second he would let go, in the hope that this would be it, that he would die and be done with all this suffering. No person should ever have to endure such torture.

Maybe it was his strong resolve that kept him going. Maybe it was his powerful body, which had now faded to almost nothing, that helped him through. Maybe it was a higher power at work.

Whatever it was, Blake Solomon made it through, and now rests in peace, but alive, unaware that his life is about to change.

CHAPTER I

~ *Their Stories* ~

Rebecca: Throughout my whole life I have never known love. I have been from foster home to foster home, to the streets and back again. From as early as I can remember, I have experimented with drugs, alcohol, and sex, trying to find acceptance in such a cruel and selfish world. Many times I thought I had found what love is, but I soon realised that men are only after one thing and they'll say or do anything to get it.

Often I thought my life was getting together—I'd find friends and become clean, and then something terrible would happen. I've been verbally, physically and sexually abused—often by the people I thought I could trust, including one of my foster dads.

The only time I ever feel safe is when I get high. Drugs know how to take away my pain. They give me peace and make me forget my worries. I feel like I'm floating, and nothing or no one can get me. If drugs are meant to be so bad then why do they make me feel so good?

I have become so blind by my addiction that I cannot see the harmful effects drugs are having on me. I used to be a smart kid, addicted to reading any and every book I could get my hands on.

Now I'm addicted to something terrible. My brain is fried and my body is fading away to nothing. When I can't get my stuff, I come down hard, vomiting and shitting all over the place til it's all out of my body.

My life is over. Finished.

Oh well, I guess nothing worse can possibly happen to me. Could it?

I have ended up in this place, this room. I don't even know how I got here. I don't remember. Or perhaps I don't want to remember. I don't even know where I am, sometimes even who I am. This room holds many painful memories I am sometimes able to forget but that often come flooding back to me and I scream and punch the walls until I collapse.

It is dull, with no window, the only light is from a small lamp with a pale red globe. The dim light shines on the pale pink walls—at least I think they're pink, I haven't seen the walls in proper daylight. There are only a few pieces of furniture in this room—a large king-sized bed with satin sheets and a wardrobe are the main items. There is a cracked mirror behind the bed with a curtain to hide it if unwanted. A small bedside table holds my only possessions in this world—a small photo of a family I don't even recognise, three tatted books that I've read dozens of times, a glass vase with no flowers and a key that I have no idea what's for.

There is a knock on the door.

My heart sinks for I know what's on the other side.

A well-built man enters. His skin looks leathery from too many days in the sun. As he gets closer I am hit by the horrible stench of stale booze, cigarettes and day-old sweat. He grins at me with his crooked, tobacco stained teeth.

"Allo sweet'art. You've got a nice tight lookin' bum there." He winks at me.

Any normal person would cringe at the sight of him, not to mention the smell. I don't even notice. It doesn't matter anymore. They're all the same—each one as dirty as the last.

They pay more for the younger girls.

I used to care, but now it's become my way of life. It's what I know. It's all I know.

I stare at the cracks in the ceiling. I count them for the millionth time.

There is another knock on the door—this man's time is up.

My dinner is placed on the ground. I place it on my bed and sit by it, staring at the same meal I have eaten for what seems like an eternity. Today I notice something new—a small cupcake and a tiny card that reads—"Happy 17th birthday Bec. X."

Wow. How generous of *him*.

Next to the food is a small tray with a syringe in it. They give us drugs to help us escape.

I want to escape for good.

I reach under my bed and pull out a bowl that I have been keeping these substance-filled syringes in, storing them up for over a week. I never know what's in them. Sometimes smack, other times it's crack, and on special occasions I get something completely out of control. It doesn't matter what's in them now.

My stash should do the job.

The most difficult part was going cold-turkey so that I could save up enough of the drugs. I got a lot of complaints this week, being too sick to perform. I've got the bruises to prove it.

I take one last look at my prison. I'll be glad to escape from here.

The photo of the family I never knew stares up at me. I think that's me to the left of the woman, perhaps my mother—the toddler clutching the doll. I guess I'll never know for sure.

I inject needle after needle into my scarred veins until my mind and body relax into a state of ecstasy.

I lie back on the bed and stare at the ceiling, the cracks slowly disappear, and the room turns bright white before fading to black.

Jason: "Come back here you piece of shit!" I yell furiously at a member from a rival gang. We were supposed to meet to strike a deal and discuss a truce but it went pear-shaped when they tried to double-cross us. A massive fight erupted—fists, baseball bats, chains, and knives—the lot. My crew were outnumbered but still much stronger and the other gang members still standing started running. Of course we had to give chase. Nobody gets away with messing with my crew.

Nobody.

Most of the enemy crew managed to escape in their cars but a few were still trying to get away on foot. I chose the meanest, strongest looking bloke to chase—it's only fair. Being the best fighter in my crew and by far the scariest looking intimidates even the toughest guys. My well-built, tattooed body has many scars—remnants of the fierce battles I have fought to protect my own and my territory. Far too many for any nineteen year-old. Those who caused the scars came worse off, believe me.

This guy would be my next victim. I've never actually killed anyone but I do a good enough job on them to make them wish they were dead. Some never walk again.

I haven't always been like this—a violent gang-member. I was the eldest child in a nice Christian family—Church every Sunday, that sort of thing. I had two younger brothers, and my sister was the youngest. My parents were great. They were supportive and helped me while I studied Law at University. I was the youngest in my class, having been advanced a couple of years throughout school. I had an amazing girlfriend who I had planned to marry. I was the captain of the University football team. Everything was fantastic until the day when my family was murdered by a vicious Negro gang. This notorious gang killed four innocent people—*my* family.

They slaughtered them all while they slept, and just because my dad was a top cop who had led a big bust on them, putting most in jail. They were murdered, and I wasn't there to protect them. I cannot even describe the intense rage that boiled up inside me that fateful day. All I could see was red. A primal need for revenge arose inside me and everything in my world was changed forever.

That was the day I decided to join a gang and hunt the killers down.

And I did.

They are now all in jail, two of them paraplegics.

I follow the thug up an alleyway in between two run-down apartment blocks and see him disappear around a corner.

I round the corner just as the thug is pulling out his gun causing me to skid to a halt.

The thug's hand is quivering—it reminds me of the first time I shot someone and the rush of adrenaline coursing through my veins. The only difference is I've never shot to kill.

"Don't do it bro, it's not worth it…" I try reasoning with him but my voice is lost through the echo of a single gunshot.

Felicity: *How do I feel right now?* I don't even know how I feel and I wouldn't tell you if I did.

It feels like this whole world is ganging up on me, crushing me under its weight. I can't seem to do anything right in anyone's eyes. My parents have always expected so much of me and I've always delivered, up until recently of course. Rather than trying my best to impress I have rebelled in every teenage way possible and worse. I've become the town's wildest party-animal, a self-inflicted reputation which seems to create more trouble than any temporary fix. I have been welcomed into a dark underworld, inescapable, always meeting with new and dangerous people, flirting with sure disaster.

If only I were brave enough to actually tell you all this, rather than the lies.

After my meeting with Doctor Bryant, the chauffeured vehicle takes me home to my parents' three-story townhouse. They started my therapy sessions after my straight-A grades dropped rapidly. They think this resulted from the stress caused by my younger brother Ben dying but I don't know. We knew he was going to die so I thought I was ready. Maybe I wasn't.

Whatever.

I walk up to my room after mumbling something to my mum who doesn't even look up from her computer. My dad isn't home as usual. Probably out with one of his secretaries, or away on a "business trip". Is mum really that naïve? I guess as long as the big-bucks keep rolling in she'll stay put. Until her fashion magazine takes off that is.

Today at school three guys asked me out. Wow. Can't I go just one day without being pursued? It'd be nice to find a guy worthy of pursuing. I haven't found one as yet though. Bianca sat with me at lunch. She's really nice and really pretty. Maybe I will go to her party this weekend and drown my sorrows.

What have I got to feel sorry for? I don't know. I don't know why I feel all of these feelings. One minute I'll be happy and smiling and cracking jokes—usually at school around my friends as a front, and the next minute I'll be so down that I'll think of numerous different ways to end my life. Sometimes when I'm feeling low I'll intentionally cause a fight with one of my closest friends or my mum because for some reason it makes me feel better—it's like a boost of energy better than a sugar-high. Especially when we make up. I love that feeling. I crave it.

I crave those rare moments when suddenly, for no explicit reason I feel on top of the world, like I can conquer anything. I often rush around planning exciting new outings with friends, sit with mum and give her ideas for her magazine, and even go out into public feeling a new air of confidence.

All of this is shattered when the depression sets in.

Being extremely depressed can be dangerous. You forget all the times when life seemed to be on track with nothing to fret about and you ignore the personal promises you made never to hurt yourself again.

Right now is one of those times.

I stand next to my mirror and pull the sweatbands from my wrist to reveal my many scars—the true face of my feelings.

Today feels different.

I pick up my precious, trustworthy razor blade and look down at my wrists.

But something is different. The urge to cut my wrists is no longer there. I no longer feel as if I need to cut them in order to feel better about myself, which in actual fact makes me feel worse and causes a vicious downward spiral. I also no longer feel the need to take any drugs to pick me up again, so I leave my stash alone.

I must be getting better.

The therapy sessions must be working.

But *why* do I feel different today? *What* is it that feels different?

It hurts inside. Something deep, deeper than usual, is eating away at me, gnawing me to the core.

I look up at my face and see the darkness in the normally bright blue eyes, the damp cheeks from crying and the sad mouth that hasn't smiled truthfully for years.

My heart is pounding. I feel the veins in my neck throbbing hard and I look at them.

Suddenly my mind is clear of any irrational or confused thoughts. My heart is no longer aching and the persistent sick feeling inside me is gone.

I bring the blade up to my throat.

It's over. *I am free.*

Matthew: I'm sick of running. I'm sick of hiding. I'm sick and tired of all the terrible things that happen on this earth. Every single day I shed tears at the horrible way we treat one another. Living on the streets means I am watching my back all the time and have to sleep with one eye open. Some days are better than others. I like the days when I am able to get to the shelter in time and have a nice hot meal, a shower and a warm bed to sleep in. These nights I can catch up on weeks of broken sleep and my body can relax for once. The line-up to the shelter has been getting even longer lately. Maybe I'm just arriving later. Or perhaps the other shelters are closing down. Whatever it is, I seem to be missing out a lot more. It sucks.

We used to all get along. Homeless people had this code where we respected and were good to one another. If someone was sick, pregnant or old, another person would give up their bed for a night for them, or offer them some food. We would share what little belongings we had. It didn't matter where we had come from or why we were poor, everyone treated each other the same.

Shops around the area would help us out. Bakeries would leave unsold bread in bags out the back alley for us to take. The supermarket would give us nearly expired goods in return for a few easy jobs such as trolley collecting. I would go to the library everyday to read and practice my English. A local chemist would also sometimes help us out with medicine if needed.

Not anymore.

Something changed in this town. A new mayor came in and suddenly the locals were no longer interested in helping us out. Thanks to his campaign to "clean up the streets" we have to be more careful about where we live, sleep and even walk as we are now hated. It wasn't only the homeless that were affected though. I used to attend a local Catholic Church—a place where I have never felt more welcome. A month after the new mayor arrived, the Church was torn down to make room for a hotel. The few African families who happily lived here were driven out with no compensation. Now we're slowly but surely being driven out too.

We used to live in peace and very rarely had to break the law to get by. Without the kindness of most of the townspeople, this did not last long.

I've been stealing for two months now to survive. Usually I resort to stealing only food so I don't starve but recently I've been trying to steal clothes so that I can walk around without looking like a hobo.

Many of my homeless buddies have been killed trying to steal food, or have ended their own lives because it has all become too hard. The murders were declared as self-defence so the offenders have gotten away with it. Last week, Alan was put into jail for retaliating to a baseball-bat wielding man who was laying into him for trying to steal an apple, which had fallen off a tree onto the footpath.

Today I am starving. I haven't eaten proper food in two weeks and I haven't eaten completely in two days. My gut feels like it is feasting on itself, and my body feels heavier than a slab of cement. If it weren't for being so keen to see my family again I would probably give up and let myself die.

Due to increasing theft, most shops have new security guards and alarm systems, so we have been turning to residential buildings and gardens for food. I know that Mr. and Mrs. Larson, who own the local Fruit and Veg Store, keep a lot of their stock in a wooden shed out the back of their home. A high fence surrounds it to keep criminals out, but I have a pair of wire cutters—stolen from the hardware store earlier this week. Once inside I stare at the rows and rows of fruit and vegetables. My eyes become blurry with tears at the delicious sight. I grab an apple and eat it so fast you could say that I inhaled it. I grab a bucket that is on the ground and start filling it up while munching on a pear. I grab as many different types—I'd like a balanced diet.

I'm too carried away with my shopping spree to notice that Mr. Larson has padlocked me inside the shed.

"You're dead now you bloody thief!"

My heart stops. Mr. Larson is rich enough not to care about his stock of produce and begins to pour petrol onto the outside of the wooden shed. I run to the other end to find another way out but with no luck.

I grab a spade and frantically try to lever a plank of wood away just as the place bursts into flames burning everything inside.

CHAPTER 2

~ *First Encounter* ~

Felicity: My God, what am *I* doing here? I don't want to be in some pointless rehab program! I thought rehab was for serious drug addicts. Apparently this isn't that type of place. Apparently this is for people with numerous other problems. I guess it'll be just like my sessions with Doctor Bryant. I'll just make up crap like I always do and they'll sign me off as sane and set me free back to my same old depressing life. I look around the room and see three others—two guys, not much older than me and a girl who looks about the same age.

The last thing I remember about being in hospital was waking up one day to see my parents standing with a couple of doctors. My mum was crying and being held by my dad. I had cords going into me and a heart monitor on. I don't even remember how I got there or anything else that happened. Apparently I have amnesia. More like I don't want to remember anything.

I wish I didn't remember anything...

The flashbacks are crippling.

The guy running the show walks in and plonks his briefcase down on the large wooden desk at the front of the room. He looks a bit like George Clooney, even has the stubble, but with a few more streaks of grey in his hair. He admires everybody in the room with a peculiar grin on his face.

I know I'm going to hate this already.

"Hi everyone, my name is Blake Solomon. How are we all?"

Complete silence. Nice try buddy.

"That's okay, we'll have plenty of time to loosen up and have some fun in the meantime. Let's get the boring formalities out of the way—welcome to Another Chance at Life. We say *another* chance, as many people have had numerous chances, while others are less fortunate. You, my friends, are the lucky ones. Many people have passed away from a lot less than what you guys went through, so I'm guessing the Big Boss up top needs you here for a little while longer. Whether you want to count your lucky stars, whatever the reason is, your new life can begin now. I'll provide the groundwork but it's up to you where you go from here."

Yeah, whatever loser.

Blake examines the confused and angry faces in the room. Not one of them is giving him eye contact. He passes around some booklets and some name tags for the four to wear. I don't even look up or thank him when he passes me mine.

He touches my arm gently. "It'll be okay Felicity."

I frown and look up at him and notice the kindness in his eyes. This is obviously a man who has never hurt a fly, or a very good imposter. Keep my guard up.

"Seeing as you have already had a lot explained to you before you came here I won't bore you with any more details. But I have put together a short film to get the ball rolling that will explain a bit of the history of this place, as well as myself. And we'll learn a lot more about each other over the coming weeks."

Blake presses play and the enormous LCD television screen springs to life with a panning shot of the clinic. A female voice begins to speak over the fading music.

"...Not all are lucky enough to get a second chance at life— even the sinful deserve one... Another Chance at Life is a healing program aimed at youths experiencing a crisis. The centre is based here at Anchor Beach due to the healing qualities of the beautiful surrounding natural environment, and also because we are able to use the refurbished Anchor Beach Psychiatric Hospital established here in the early 1900s."

The screen shot changes from spectacular views of the building surrounded by beautiful landscapes and the coastline, to footage from the news.

"When the program first began in 2007, there were many obstacles, including one very tragic incident resulting in the destruction of half the facility. Many of the children involved were injured or received severe burns, and the program was consequently shut down."

Oh great, I'm stuck here in this desolate shit-hole with a guy who doesn't even know what he is doing.

"Since then, Blake Solomon, the founder, has worked with authorities and the community to rebuild this innovative and positive program. With a PhD in Psychology, Blake is a man with the vision to do whatever it takes to save troubled youths from their destructive lives. The program's contents range from group discussions, guest speakers, and one-on-one therapy sessions, to fun activities like water sports, camping, and games nights. We hope you will strive to benefit from your time here and are able to make some serious changes to yourselves and your lives."

What a load of bollocks. I can't believe my parents are allowing these people to hold me in this prison and forced to listen to this bullshit. It's obvious this place is a cult and they'll try to brainwash us. Well I for one won't be letting that happen. I quickly glance at Blake as he switches the TV off and notice that he's still smiling. What a quack. He turns suddenly and catches my eye so I quickly look away.

"The idea of this program is to help you overcome all of the traumatic events that have happened leading up to you being here," Blake continues his mind-numbingly boring explanation.

I don't know where he gets off thinking he can help us. He doesn't even know us! And who cares if he's got the experience in this sort of thing, it doesn't mean he's truly interested in helping *us*.

"It is a voluntary program, so you are free to leave if you wish."

Why didn't you say so earlier!

"However, leaving will unfortunately incur consequences as you have all broken the law in one way or another. Consider this program as a means to wipe the slate clean and to start anew. And besides, the closest town Is a good two hour drive from here, so probably not the best idea to run away."

He says this as if he knows we'll try.

"A bus will come once a week with any visitors and supplies that we need."

Blake finally registers the tension in the room.

"Relax guys. Think of this as a holiday, with a bit of life-coaching on the side. Are there any questions?"

"Yeah." The skin-head across the room sits bolt-upright, glaring at Blake. Boy he looks pissed off! "What makes you think we wanna be here and listen to this shit?"

Blake takes a sip of his coffee and leans back in his chair slightly to try and relax the atmosphere.

"Of course you don't *want* to be here. Nobody does. Not right now. But you will, trust me."

"Why the hell should I trust you? I don't even know you! You look like every other god-damn arsehole out there. And did you really think showing us some stupid video to make you look good will make us just do what you say? You're dreaming buddy."

"Jason," Blake says calmly. "It's okay to be scared mate."

This comment just seems to piss Jason off even more. Blake seems way out of his depth here. It's kind of funny to watch.

"Believe me, I've seen it all before," Blake continues. "Not long ago I was scared like you are now. I was given another chance just like you guys, and I am using my opportunity the best way I know—helping others. I won't preach to you. I'll just listen to you, offer you advice and you're grown up enough to take it from there. I swear I won't force anything upon you, and I won't let you down. I promise."

"Yeah? What would you know about a hard life? My life?"

"I'm not saying I would even begin to understand what you've been through Jason. Or any of you for that matter. But we've all got stories to tell here so I'll ask you to respect that."

Jason glares at Blake with a fighting-stare and waves it off.

"Now, you've all been given your rooms right?"

There are a couple of nods.

"Excellent. Feel free to explore the resort, and I will see you all at dinner."

Rebecca: Thank goodness that was quick—I hate these group things. I hate being around people I don't know, and I hate sharing any of my life with anyone else. I'll be the quiet one of the group. They can't force me to talk if I don't want to. I'll say a couple of things to make them all feel sorry for me and then say it's too hard for me to talk about it. Yeah I'll play that card. But it's going to be hard to keep that up for however long this rehab takes. As I leave the room I bump into one of the other guys, Jason I think. He mutters "bitch" and keeps walking. God I hate men. The very sight of them makes my stomach churn. I'd be happy if I never saw one again, pieces of shit.

Hmmm, I could really do with a hit of scag right about now. It's been too long and I crave it so much my head spins.

I quickly walk outside to get some fresh air and my ill feeling immediately goes.

Whoa.

This is the first time I have actually properly looked at where we're staying—we only arrived an hour ago, after sleeping the whole bus-trip and were bustled straight into the main hall.

This beach is amazing! I've never been to a beach before. My first foster dad took his own kids all through summer but always left me to clean up the house. I never argued for fear of another beating. I always thought I deserved to be treated like this for some reason, but to this day have never figured out why. There must be something wrong with me seeing as nobody wants me. Being treated like shit was the only attention I ever got from my foster families. I think I liked that kind of attention over being ignored so I used to muck up and be a little brat. They even sent me to the cheapest school they could find thinking I was stupid. Little did they know that those nights I came home late I was spending in the library. Before my foster dad removed the lock to my room, I could feel safe behind the locked door and read til my eyes were exhausted and sore. I never got distracted from the banging on the door and the threats made. I knew I had to open it eventually, and took the beatings I knew I deserved. I had a pretty thick skin, but eventually the physical, emotional and sexual abuse broke me.

Argh! Shut-up!

I hit myself in the head to stop the thoughts. My mind goes crazy like this. A million miles a second and there's no way I can distract myself from it. Until now.

This beach is far better than I had imagined—although I always imagined it from cartoons I had seen when I was younger and photos in books from the library. I can't believe how real and beautiful it is. I can actually reach out and touch it, smell it, taste it. There's just so much to take in all at once—the soft sand and huge dunes, to the enormous ocean, and even the sea air blows me away with its freshness. The beach stretches all the way around a beautiful bay and we've got the whole place to ourselves! I feel like my insides are ready to explode with joy. A worker from the resort walks past so I quickly hide my excitement.

Maybe this could be the place. I failed last time, but never again. I'll make sure of it this time.

The crystal clear water lapping effortlessly onto the flawless white sand is like nothing I could ever have imagined. It's perfect. As if I deserve any of this.

Felicity: I can't believe I'm stuck in this hell-hole for God knows how many weeks or months! A resort he said? It's a stupid ugly shack on a beach, so far away from civilisation it's surprising they have electricity. And where is my mobile phone? I'm sure all my friends are trying to contact me. Oh who cares anyway? They're all pretentious snobs, just trying to use me. I can't find any decent trustworthy friends and that's not going to change anytime soon so I better keep my guard up in this place. The guy with tattoos was kinda cute though. Rough, but cute...

Hey what the hell am I saying?! Not only do I *not* want to talk to anyone or get to know anyone or even listen to anyone, but a guy like that wouldn't be interested in me anyway. Unless he knew how rich I was of course. That's all my other friends care about. They're there for me when I have a new phone, or car, or hold a party but never when I'm sick. Those friends who I buy expensive presents for with my dad's credit card are nowhere to be found when I need them most.

I walk outside and see the other girl in the group standing on the beach. She sees me, looks down and quickly walks the other way. She has nice, long blonde hair and a pretty face, but very pale, sickly looking skin. Plus she is way too thin—maybe she's anorexic. I stare at her intrigued until she disappears and I focus my attention back on the hideous shanty I have to call home for four long weeks. What a waste of my time.

The main building is a two-story beach house that is in need of a good paintjob. There are a few other buildings behind it, which I can't be bothered exploring. I think I saw a pool earlier—that kind of defeats the purpose of being at the beach though doesn't it? The front porch has stairs that literally lead straight onto the beach. Something distracts me and I realise that the dressing on my neck is beginning to come off so I walk inside to find the nurse.

Matthew: Man, I don't want to stay here for this rehab. I wonder if I can somehow move here forever! I've never stayed in anywhere nearly as nice as this place. It's awesome! My room has a balcony to walk out onto with a couch to sit and admire the view of the beach. I am a little bit overwhelmed by it all. This is the first time in my life that I've ever had my own room. My own room! This room is all *mine*! Even though it is only mine for the program, I just cannot believe it. I really don't care what I have to do during this rehab program because I'd do anything for a place like this. Everyone else didn't seem like they wanted to be here. The other guy in the group, the skinhead, stared me down earlier on and I smiled back but he just said—"What the hell are you staring at?" It was obvious that he was the one staring but I decided not to point that out. I grab my bag and proceed to put away my things. The first thing I grab is my pair of board-shorts, stolen from a clothes line earlier this year. I then place a singlet in the draw, two pairs of undies and socks, and a necklace with a cross—belonging to my mother. Well that was easy, and just look at all the space I have left! I heard them say there are plenty of spare clothes if we need them, but I'm pretty sure this isn't meant to be a fashion parade. I chuckle to myself and immediately cringe at the stabbing pain in my side. It could've been worse I guess. I heard them say that anyone who received injuries and burns of this severity should be dead. I'll be getting further treatment here—there's a resident nurse and doctor who comes twice a week and on call. Apparently I'm recovering really well though. Someone remarked at how tough and resilient I am—if only they knew why. You have to be tough to survive where I grew up.

I don't remember much of what happened, but I do remember waking up several times a day and looking at the empty chair and table next to my hospital bed hoping to see a visitor or some flowers or a card. I think that loneliness cut me deeper than the wounds in my side. Anyone who did come to visit probably would've been scared off by the police officer guarding my door. I guess they thought I lit the fire, I'm not too sure, but I didn't even have to show up in court and I was whisked away here as soon as I became well enough. But I'm not complaining! I love this place already! I hope I can make some friends though.

I sigh as I grab my crutches and head downstairs for dinner.

Jason: I am already sick of this place. Why does everyone stare at me? What am I doing here? What the hell do they want from me? I've tried my best to set my life straight but it never works out. And so what if I got shot! I didn't get killed so who really cares? Nobody has ever truly cared about me, even when my family was murdered. They were the only people that mattered in my life. They loved me no matter what mistakes I made. Oh God, I can feel the anger building again. My blood boils every time I think about that fateful day when my life was torn apart forever. This is the exact anger that drew me to the violent ways of gang life. Nothing has changed since that moment and nothing ever will. Being stuck in this place only makes me angrier and I want to, need to escape.

I walk upstairs to my room and pass the other guy in my group who is staring at me again. Didn't he get the message last time? He's obviously not the smartest kid. I tell him to piss off and help him down the stairs with a hard shove—he falls flat on his face, sucker. Doesn't he know who I am and what I'm capable of? Nobody stares at me where I'm from, unless they're looking for trouble. Even then they end up regretting it when I show them a glimpse of the rage deep inside of me. Maybe I should show him. If he keeps staring at me I'll kick his bloody teeth in—to begin with. I even caught one of the girls staring at me earlier on. Not interested sorry love. She looks like a prissy little bitch anyway with her perfectly straightened, high-lighted hair and flawless tanned skin. Ok I admit she is very good-looking, as in super hot but like I said—I'm not interested! She wears too much makeup anyway. As if *she* has anything to hide.

On the way to my room I notice a common room. It has a pool table in it and some couches sitting opposite a widescreen TV. That's a good sign—at least I'll be able to spend my time in here rather than with those losers. I walk into the bathroom and stare into the mirror. Under my singlet, the left side of my chest is still strapped up from the surgery—the doctor says he will take the stitches out next week. The bullet stopped in my lung causing it to collapse and I'm lucky to be here the doctor said. An inch to the right and it would've hit my heart or large blood vessels. Too bad it didn't. I'd love any chance to see my family again, even if it means dying. Yes, I mean it. But I'd never take my life. No, that'd be the easy way out of all my problems. Yes I said it, I have problems. It still doesn't explain why I'm in this shit of a place.

Another chance at life hey?

Whatever.

I don't want another chance. I'm not going to change. Ever.

CHAPTER 3

~ Group Session ~

"What on earth is that?" Blake asks as he walks briskly down the hallway, his assistant in tail. There is a loud crashing noise coming from the conference room. Blake rushes in to see Jason laying hard kicks into Matthew who is on the ground. The kicks are so violent and forceful that the sound of cracking ribs fills the air.

"I'll get security," Blake's assistant says as she rushes off.

Chairs scattered around the place are evidence of the tussle, and Matthew is huddled into a ball trying to protect his head and his wounds. It is already obvious that Jason has aggravated the wounds, with blood seeping through the delicate skin grafts. Blake drops his briefcase spilling its contents and grabs Jason by his shirt collar, lifts him up and drops him onto his back on a table. Jason tries to get up but Blake clasps his enormous calloused right hand on Jason's collarbone and easily keeps him from moving.

"Get him to the nurse!" Blake shouts to the girls who immediately rush over and help Matthew up. Blake turns to Jason.

"What the hell are you playing at?"

"He wouldn't stop staring at me! And get your filthy paws off me before I tear you apart!"

Blake tightens his grip.

"Careful Jason." Blake's well-trained gigantic biceps, and equally huge forearms barely need to flex to hold Jason in place. "Don't bring this nonsense here okay?"

Blake slowly lets Jason go once he is calm. Jason starts rubbing his neck, sending a deathly gaze at Blake.

"You can't touch me! You're a dead man!" Jason's face is red as he shouts furiously at Blake.

"You just attacked an injured and defenceless man Jason." Blake's voice remains steady and calm. "I'll convince him not to press charges if you promise to cut out this crap."

Jason nods but continues to breathe heavily and step from side to side, fists clenched as if preparing for a fight. The clinic's lone security guard strolls in casually and winks knowingly at Blake, who nods back.

"Now take a minute to calm down while I go to see if Matthew is ok."

Blake turns quickly and walks away.

"Dirty nigger," Jason mumbles as Blake exits the room, stopping him in his tracks. After a pause, Blake turns steadily around to face Jason.

"What did you just say?"

"I wasn't talking to you." Jason's eyes are dark with hatred.

Blake's steady and piercing gaze is enough to burn through the defences of even the toughest of men.

"Don't you *ever* say anything like that again, in this place or anywhere else. That is *unacceptable*."

"What is? Nigger? That's what he is isn't he? A dirty, rotten, scumbag, piece of shit nigger." Jason spits at the ground after he says the last word. Years of hatred and disgust couldn't be changed or taken away just like that.

Jason gets in Blake's face. "And who the hell are you to tell me what to do?"

Blake doesn't budge.

"What are *you* gonna do huh?" Jason scowls. So much hatred. So much anger. "You can't hurt me! I'll kill you! I'll kill you all!"

"Calm down Jason." Blake looks at him sincerely. "I would never hurt you. I am here to help you. But I can't help you if you act like this."

Blake puts a reassuring hand on Jason's shoulder, which is promptly swept away.

"I don't need your help," Jason says as he turns and walks away.

"Yes you do. And you know it."

Jason takes a seat and stares out of the window.

"I hate this place."

"I know you do Jason. You may hate it now. But you won't regret it. Trust me." Blake's face is soft with integrity.

"And why should I trust you?" Jason does not relax his clenched fists.

"Because you don't want to go back to your old life. It's not worth it. This may be your last chance to become a better person, not only for yourself, but for your baby daughter."

Jason's eyes shoot up to meet Blake's.

"How do you know...?"

Blake smiles and shrugs. "I've done my research. Don't underestimate the power of the things that can take place here Jason. Amazing things can happen in your life if you let them."

"Whatever. Wanker." Jason smirks and stares back out of the window.

"Now, I'm going to get the others and we can attempt to begin our first session ok?"

Jason ignores the question but Blake's gleaming eyes persist until a response.

"Ok, whatever tough guy."

Blake exits and heads to the clinic where the nurse is finishing up re-dressing Matthew's wounds.

"How ya doing champ? That was some beating."

"I've had worse." Matthew smiles and gets up too quickly, hesitating to allow time for the sharp pains in his side to soothe.

"That's the spirit. Are you sure you want to go on with this today? You can always sit this session out if you like."

"Why should Matthew have to miss out?" Felicity asks, her face intense and scowling. "Jason's the one who should be banned. He should be locked up, the thug."

"Nah, let's just get on with it." Matthew rests a firm reassuring hand on Felicity's arm. Her look of a toddler about to have a tantrum fades.

Blake and Matthew lead the way back to the room, the entrance still being guarded. Jason glares at Matthew as he sits down opposite him, this time avoiding eye contact. The girls also sit further away from Jason this time.

"Ok," Blake begins. "Let me just set something straight. Anything that goes on in here stays in here. Anything that any one of us says or does remains within this group. With this safety and confidence we will be able to freely express our true opinions and really get something from these sessions. Is that clear with everyone?"

Everyone nods except for Jason who is still alternating between throwing scathing glares at Matthew and staring longingly out the window.

"In a moment I will show you the movie, *Freedom Writers*, which I believe you'll relate to in some way. That will begin our discussion point for today, which is living with adversity."

Blake passes around a copy of one of his books *The Angels*.

"I want you all to read this book in your own time and keep in mind that it is based on the true stories of young people just like you. Now, has anyone seen the movie *Freedom Writers*?"

Everyone shakes their head, apart from Jason who does not respond again.

"Alright, let's get it started then!"

Blake starts the DVD, turns off the lights and pulls the window blinds down to darken the room—Jason glares at Blake for doing this.

Throughout the film, Blake notices that Felicity looks interested but sad at some points, Rebecca looks terrified and confused, Matthew looks angry but then relieved and happy by the end, and Jason looks uninterested but actually watches the whole film.

"So, what were your feelings about this movie?" Blake asks the group as he reopens the blinds and switches the lights back on.

Rebecca: Oh God, please don't pick me! If I keep staring at the ground and avoid eye-contact then maybe he won't pick me. I have no idea how I felt about that movie. To be honest, I was actually excited about seeing it because I cannot remember the last movie I saw. And besides, I wouldn't have a clue how it related to me, to my life. Those kids were lucky compared to what I've been through! They have no idea what real pain and suffering is! I wish my problems could be solved as easily as theirs were. At least their teacher truly cared for them—the only time anyone takes an interest in me is for sex or money or both.

"Rebecca?"

Oh crap, he's asking me. That's just typical.

"What did you think about the movie?"

I glance up at him briefly, brave a trembling smile and shrug feebly before dropping my eyes back to the floor. My heart is racing, my face is burning and I feel like everyone in the room is watching me. I hate this place! I need to get out of here! I need my pills. I need my escape. Oh God help me!

Just let me die.

Felicity: What a wimp. I look at her and shake my head, which I think Blake notices because he asks me next.

"I enjoyed the movie because I got to see how less-fortunate kids live and go to school and it made me realise just how lucky I am. I feel sorry for those kids."

That certainly came out easier than I thought it would. Blake seemed okay with my answer. If I keep this up I'll be out of here sooner than I know it!

I don't even notice my lies anymore—they just flow so naturally with my normal conversation they avoid being noticed by the best lie-detectors. If only they knew what I really thought...

I'm not lucky at all.

I hate my life. I hate everyone and everything in it. Especially myself.

I'd trade lives with any of those kids.

Matthew: Lucky?! She doesn't even care, or even know how lucky she is! Rich little cow. She doesn't care about kids like the ones in the movie—kids like me. What a manipulative bitch. The only thing she's sorry about is that she isn't in her mansion watching her fifty-thousand inch TV and being waited on by her slave!

Oh great, my turn to give an opinion. If only I really could say how I feel. I don't want to lie, I'm not very good at it.

"It was good. I think I've seen movies like that, but I liked this one better because it was a true story."

I cannot believe I just lied like that! I guess I feel like I have to hide my true self in front of these people for fear of rejection. They would never accept me for who am I. I shouldn't really care about that though—it's happened most of my life, being shunned for who I am.

Yes it is true, I did enjoy the movie. Of course I did. How could I not enjoy it? It was the first movie I've ever seen in my life.

Jason: What a scumbag. I bet he loves the fact that the girls took him to the nurse's room and gave him all that attention. My fist is begging to give him some more attention. He better watch himself. One wrong word, one lingering look, that's all it will take to push me over the edge. Just look at him! He makes me sick. I bet the jeans and t-shirt he's wearing are stolen. Yeah, I *bet* you've seen movies like that before. You've probably watched stolen DVDs on your stolen TV, sitting on your stolen couch in your stolen house! Yeah that's right mate, avoid eye-contact with me. I'll get you, and you know it. You lowly worthless piece of shit...

"Jason! For the third time, do you have anything to add to this discussion?"

How dare he shout my name! Blasphemy! I've had enough of this.

"How about you all go to hell," I declare calmly but sternly as I get up and storm out whilst flipping the bird.

"Jason!" Blake calls out desperately to me but I slam the door behind me.

"Well I think that will do us for now," Blake says, a bit shaken. "The rest of you have some activities with Brenda and then some free time til tomorrow at two pm when we'll meet for our one-on-one sessions. Don't forget to have a look at the kitchen and cleaning roster, which also starts tomorrow. Are there any questions?"

After a brief silence, Blake waits for the remainder to leave before heading to the main office. He enters without knocking and marches over to the startled lady behind the desk and plants a large kiss on her lips.

"Mmm, what was that for?" The lady grins widely at Blake.

"Because you're my wife, my boss, my best friend, and I love you!"

"Hey I'm not complaining! How'd the first group session go?"

Blake's smile fades, replaced with a troubled expression.

"They're not responding very well, Anne. I can tell they're not interested and want to leave as soon as possible. Do you think this was a bad idea? There's already a lot of tension in the group."

"Darling, don't give up already!" Anne puts a reassuring hand on Blake's forearm. "You've only just begun."

"Yes but I can't help but be reminded about last time. This is how it all began—so much anger and resentment in such young minds, and putting them all together was the catalyst."

"You've got to stop blaming yourself sweetie. You know very well what went wrong last time, and those staff members no longer work here." Anne places a soft hand on Blake's stubbled chin. "You know what your job is and you know you're very capable of achieving anything you set your mind on. Give them a chance and they'll open up. They need you to stay strong…"

Anne is interrupted by Blake's sudden and fierce coughing fit.

"Are you okay sweetie? Shall I get your medicine?"

"I'm fine, thanks," Blake says as he catches his breath. "They all just look so lost. I can see it in their eyes. I just don't know how I can get through to them, and they don't seem to want to talk. And when they are talking, they're not saying much or they're not being truthful. I know it hasn't been long but it's like they're scared to face the truth or ashamed to reveal things to the group. I need another way... Something less intimidating."

Blake's face suddenly lights up.

"Why didn't I think of this before?" He gets up and walks briskly out of the office leaving a bewildered look on his wife's face.

CHAPTER 4

~ Head to Head ~

Felicity: Oh my goodness! If I have to wait here any longer I'll go crazy! Matthew has already been in to see Blake, and Rebecca is in there at the moment. Jason was supposed to go first but he is still missing from breakfast—the second time in two days he has lost his temper and disappeared. This time it was literally over spilt milk—Matthew turned and accidentally bumped into Jason, spilling his bowl of cereal. He went nuts! I thought he was going to rip Matthew's head off so I stepped in between and told him to relax. He wasn't happy with me but instead of arguing back he just took off, and we haven't seen him since. Matthew thanked me and sat down with me for a while. I can tell by the way he talks that English isn't his first language, by his accent. He's still very good though. I wonder where he's from.

We did an exercise this morning to try and get to know one another by doing mock interviews but nobody seemed interested. Blake tried his best with the three of us, but I don't think we're very compatible. It feels like Blake is just fumbling his way through this—like he's never done this type of thing before. We ended up just playing Wii together, which seemed to break the ice a little.

Blake seemed pretty excited about our one-on-one sessions this afternoon, and he's certainly making the most of them. At least all of this waiting is giving me time to get stuck into Blake's book, *The Angels*. It's actually pretty good and I think I am really enjoying it. I can relate to one of the characters in the book—a girl called Lindsay who has had everything handed to her on a platter for her entire life but still feels empty and lost, trying to fill the void with drugs and alcohol. Oh, how I miss partying already! One thing that shocked me, and I'm glad I've never experienced, was when Lindsay walked in on her step-father beating her mother to near-death. He turned to Lindsay and said—"You're next!"

I actually feel happy right now though. I feel like I can do anything—conquer the world. But I know that the happier I feel, the further I will fall when my depression sets in. Because of this, I'm actually scared of being happy. I'm good at covering up the lows though, which always makes them last longer and fall even deeper. Part of me wants to tell someone but a larger part knows that no-one will care. How would I begin anyway?

Rebecca leaves Blake's office and disappears quickly down the hallway.

I enter the office and take a seat opposite Blake on a very comfortable armchair, still warm from its previous occupants. Blake opens up a file with my name on it.

"Felicity Jessica Ellison. Nice name but can you lend me some syllables?" Blake jokes and I half-laugh although I do not find it very funny.

"Ok I'm just going to ask you a few questions so just answer them the best you can." Blake looks happier and more relaxed than yesterday. His questions are just like the ones Doctor Bryant asks me so I am able to answer them with ease.

I guess Blake hasn't had much experience with liars.

Blake asks a bit about my family history, schooling, friends, and my hobbies and so on. He then asks some more personal questions, to do with taking drugs, having sex and suicidal thoughts. Usually this would disturb me and I would close myself off entirely. Today I'm feeling so good about myself and life that I answer every question completely and my session lasts twice as long as the other two. It's a pity that everything Blake is writing down is all made up. Oh well.

"Very good Felicity, we can go into that more now if you like?" Blake prompts me to tell him more about my brother. "Or if you'd like to think about what we've discussed we can save it for the next session, it's up to you…"

I suddenly realise I had let my guard down and started to spill out some secrets about Ben. How could I let that happen?!

"Um, I dunno. My mind's a bit jumbled at the moment so I think I'll save it."

What was I thinking? I thought I was successfully controlling the situation. He must've tricked me into telling him! Bastard! Oh my God. Are my eyes welling up? Snap out of it!

"That's fine Felicity. You've done fine, especially for your first session. And you say that you've never had counselling before?"

I shake my head. Another lie to add to the long list. Blake almost looks amused at this reply. He knows more than I think he does hey.

"One last thing before you leave." Blake reaches behind into his desk draw and pulls out a digital video camera in a carry bag. "I've got one for all of you. I noticed that it may take a while for you guys to completely open up to one another so instead, why don't you tell your stories, thoughts, ideas, or whatever to this camera? Dance to it, sing to it, do whatever, I don't mind. During each week it will be up to you whether or not you will show the footage to the group or just to me. It's your choice. There are instructions in there on how to operate the camera so happy filming!"

Blake smiles his colossal, sparkling, semi-cheesy grin. I half-smile back and walk out clutching the carry bag still in disbelief at what just happened.

Matthew: Wow. Wow! I cannot believe my luck! It seems that this "traumatic" event of being caught in a huge fire has turned out to be my winning ticket. Not only do I have an amazing place to stay for a while, with good food, entertainment, and helpful people, but I just scored myself my very own video camera! Blake will want it back when I leave but I'm just excited about being able to use one!

I smile to myself and walk outside to find a nice spot to start filming straight away. I decide to leave my crutches behind—they seem pointless, as my legs do not even hurt anymore. The crutches just slow me down anyway. Walking along the beach, I take in all its beauty. I like the feeling of the soft sand sifting between my rough toes with crystal clear water lapping gently onto the shore, and seagulls gliding through the clear sky. I love how quiet it is here. Peaceful. It is nice to be in a peaceful place for once.

I am so taken in by the scenery I only just realise I have walked such a distance along the long beach that the resort looks like a tiny speck on the other side of the cove.

This will do.

I climb to the top of a huge sand dune and set up my camera and tripod facing the ocean. I skim through the information booklet a dozen times and finally turn the camera on—the starting buzz gives me a shiver. I'm going to be a movie star! I sit opposite the camera and press the record button.

The camera springs to life, but I don't. I just sit there with an awkward grin on my face and my eyes darting to and from the lens several times.

What the heck do I talk about? Blake said to talk about anything but I don't know where to begin. I'll just say whatever I guess. Here goes...

"Hi, my name is Maliik Abdu Ngoudjo, but here in your country I like to be called Matthew. I'm nineteen and I'm, uh, here to talk to you about my life."

That's an okay start. I guess I shouldn't stop now.

"Firstly though, how amazing is this place right? I've never seen anything like it..." I swing my body around to take in the vastness of the beautiful Australian scenery. "Okay, well I have lived here in this country for eight years and have been homeless for almost the whole time. Back in my homeland of Sudan we had to sleep with one eye open, with the war going on and everything. The town we lived in was very close to the fighting in the western region of Darfur.

The first time I shot an enemy rebel I was only six. Our army came through and armed all the villagers, no matter what age, with out-of-date weapons so that we could help with the fighting. It was then that we became real targets. The Janjaweed, as they're known back there don't have mercy on anyone. They rape, torture and kill man, woman and child. Everywhere we walked we had to be careful of landmines, the Janjaweed, bombs. One of my brothers was not so lucky with the mines one day. He was only five—he mistook it for a tin-can or something."

I pause, tears swelling my eyes as I reminisce the good times spent with my little brother. We were always so loyal to one another, and even though we fought a lot we'd always continue to go on our little adventures.

"I don't even remember what started the fighting. I guess I was brought up with it so it was all I knew. So many people were killed. The world doesn't even know what really went on. How could they when they're not even shown it?"

I shake my head. I remember asking most people I met when I first came to Australia what they thought of the fighting in Darfur. Most of them said, "What's Darfur?"

"I remember the day when the Janjaweed raided our village. Our army just ignored our cries for help and let it happen. There were thousands of them, riding through our village on horseback destroying everything and everyone they could find. My father had prepared for this day by building a hidden room under our floor. My family managed to get inside before the soldiers came. All but my sister. She had been playing in the street with some other kids and didn't make it back inside in time. Well, she actually did make it back inside. But the soldiers followed her..."

I look away into the distance and shake my head, trying to suppress the horrific images of my nine-year-old sister being raped and murdered by three cold-hearted, evil men.

"There was tiny cracks in the floorboards, where I could look through... I saw everything... They took turns... The sick mother-fu... There was nothing we could do to save her without being killed ourselves..."

I am so full of anger and hatred I think I'll explode. I want to find those evil bastards and give them what they deserve. It's so hard knowing I could've at least tried to save my sister but didn't. I'd be with her now if I did. Would that be so bad?

I've had enough—I switch the camera off to regain my composure.

I figure that's enough for today so I pack up and head back down to the resort as the sun begins to set. The amazing colours spreading across the horizon help me to forget my terrifying past for a brief moment.

I don't know what the others will think of my movie but I just can't wait to see myself on the big screen!

Rebecca: Why should Blake care so much that I'm not talking?! So what! Who really cares? It's not as if he truly cares about me and what I have to say. Nobody does. He's just doing his job. He'll get paid no matter what.

Out of all those questions he asked me I could only spit out a few words, yet he still seemed to know more about me than I know myself! It's a wonder that he's still trying. I guess he has sort of given up on me though by giving me this camera to talk to instead.

Why would *I* want to talk to a camera, and tell all my deepest, darkest secrets, and then let him, or worse still, *them*, watch it?! What the hell! Does he think I'm stupid or something? I may be quiet but I'm not dumb. Maybe I should just smash it. I could smash the camera right here on the rocks. I could drop it off this cliff onto the rocks below and watch the crashing waves sweep it away. They'll never find the remains out here.

I know what'll happen if I start talking about the very things I've tried to ignore most of my life. There's a good reason I never talk about this kind of stuff! Why did he do it? Why did Blake have to stir things up inside me again!

I scream at the top of my lungs.

That bastard.

I'll make him regret it.

I'm miles away from the camp now. I've walked for over an hour to get here. I had to. I had to get away from there! It's driving me crazy! People are making me feel wanted by trying to talk to me, there's proper food, which is making me start to feel healthier, and the sun is actually giving my skin a bit of colour! These are all supposed to be good things right? Why don't I feel good about myself then?!

There's just so much gnawing away at me that it feels like I've swallowed a million white ants and they're crawling around under my skin and in my head. I just want one single clear thought!

"Stop it!" I scream and hit my forehead over and over to try and stop the craziness in my mind.

Who would've known that not having access to any drugs would make my mind even more confused. A thousand conflicting thoughts fight each other for a prime spot—from the terrifying first night I spent on the streets to the thrill of watching all my pain drift away after my first hit. It's hard to believe that these are the more pleasant thoughts I try to hang onto every day. They only last a second or two before being over-run and destroyed by a more powerful and disturbing memory.

I look down the cliff-face at the jagged rocks jutting up, getting pounded by the angry ocean. They remind me of my own state-of-mind, all crooked and rough—not a single one smooth enough to sit on. Every bad memory, every single awful thing that has happened to me suddenly rushes back and I feel light-headed and ill. The pain in my heart intensifies and the confusion in my mind pushes me over the edge.

That's it!

It's the only way to end all of this torment.

I must jump over the edge.

This'll give them a video to remember! I place the camera on the ground facing towards me and press the record button.

No-one can save me now.

I close my eyes and begin to slowly let my body fall.

Jason: Man, I ought to tear this place down. Burn it to the ground like those other kids did. I should finish the job and give Blake what he deserves. How dare he tell me off! He's not even a cop or anything! He's nothing. At least I got out of that stupid one-on-one crap. I don't need some gug, some loser telling me what's wrong with my life! That's all he is—a gug, a tool, an idiot, a moron.

I should get my crew to come bust me out or something. They'd be here in a flash if they knew where I was! How can I contact them though, with our phone calls being monitored and all? And how would I give directions to this shithole.

I miss the lads. I miss getting drunk with them every weekend and causing a ruckus down the local pub. I miss having them watch my back and me watch theirs. I miss the thrill of the chase, whether it be from the cops or an armed rival. I need to get back there before I lose my shit! Maybe I should steal a car. Just like I stole this… I pull out a bottle of vodka from my jacket pocket and crack the seal. The strong scent hits my nose instantly. I take a sip and my unrelenting worries seem to just disappear—dissolved into this clear but powerful booze.

I found this bottle in the kitchen when I was looking for my drink bottle. The chef, who had hidden the bottle for his own secret stash was none-the-wiser. Sounds like he's the one who should be in rehab for having a stash of alcohol while working at a place like this! Fool. Not that I care. I seriously don't give a shit anymore.

As I wander, north I think—the opposite way to the beach anyway, I begin to plot my plan of escape.

There is a bus that comes once a week, Blake mentioned, and it's due tomorrow with our first visitors. Well I've got no-one to visit me so I guess I'll use the return trip. Too easy.

For now though, I'll just get royally smashed from this sweet nectar and fall asleep on the beach or in a paddock or something. Sounds good to me! Ironically it's the only way to stay sane in a place like this.

I take a long hard swig and gasp at the sudden but satisfying fire in my throat. I shake my head to steady my vision and notice a faint figure in the distance. Who the hell is that? I quickly duck behind a bush to make sure whoever it is can't see me. I decide to get closer and see who it is so I follow the trail along the edge of the cliff, using the shrubbery as a shield. When I round the final bend I see who it is—Rebecca! Why would she be all the way up here by herself? It's miles away from the clinic. And what is she doing standing right on the edge of the cliff?

I notice that she has a video camera in her hand—I wonder where she stole that from. She looks at it for a moment, then down at the rocks. I creep as close as I can until I can faintly hear her mumbling to herself. It sounds as if she's angry at something. Her body is quivering violently, and yet it's a warm evening.

Suddenly she stops talking. Crap, maybe she heard me. She bends down and places the camera on the ground.

No, she wouldn't, would she? Surely not...

Oh bloody hell, she is!

She spreads her arms open wide like a cross and begins to topple forward... I snap out of it and run towards her as she begins to fall.

I catch her just in time by grabbing the back of her jeans.

Thank God!

As I try to pick her up she screams at me to let her go, and starts thrashing about wildly, one of her small fists connecting lightly with my cheek.

"Let me go! This is what I want! Put me down! Leave me alone!" She screams and curses at me, but I just hold her tightly until she gives up and collapses into a heap. I pick her up, cradling her in my arms and carry her away from the deadly sheer drop. I place her down on the soft grass of the nearby fields and look down at her petite, trembling body.

"What the hell were you thinking?" I begin to yell at her but realise she is bawling so I reluctantly half-wrap my arms around her. She pulls herself in closer and holds on tightly. She continues whimpering so I try to console her. "You're okay now. I've got you. It's okay."

I feel her warm tears on my chest as they soak through my thin singlet.

"Thank you," she manages to whisper.

She is shaking severely, and I can hear the fear in her soft, sweet voice.

"It's okay," I say to her as I stroke her hair to try and soothe her. I attempt to pick her up to carry her back but she clings on tighter as if to tell me to wait a while longer. We sit there in silence for at least an hour. I don't feel the need to say anything to her and vice versa.

The sun looks magnificent as it sets on the horizon.

"We can go back now," she says softly as she looks up at me. I nod in agreement and help her to her feet. That was actually very nice, not having to worry or think about anything—a rare pleasure.

"Were you following me?" Rebecca asks, her voice still shaky but returning to normal volume.

"No, I just came for a walk to think about things," I reply and suddenly my worries come rushing back so I reach for the vodka bottle and drink quickly until there's only half left.

"Whoa dude, where'd you get that?" Rebecca's eyes light up as she stares at the bottle.

"None of your business." I glare at her and hug the precious bottle to my chest.

"Can I have some? Please?" Her face looks up at me pleadingly.

I roll my eyes and pass her the bottle. She drinks it like it is water and I doubt whether her tiny body could handle much alcohol. However, I don't see any reason why she can't get drunk with me. I'm sure she needs to drown her sorrows as well. I wonder how many times she has been drunk before. We stroll on back to the resort, and I can feel myself getting very tipsy already. It doesn't take long for the normally shy and quiet Rebecca to become very talkative. For the first time since I arrived at this horrible place I had a decent, even though drunken conversation.

CHAPTER 5

~ *Confused* ~

Felicity: I still don't understand exactly what happened today in my session with Blake. He asked some really simple questions—ones I've answered before with Doctor Bryant, but for some reason he actually got through to me this time. He somehow penetrated my normally invincible barrier and I actually started to be honest with him. I'm not sure why. Maybe it was because he was being sincere and actually cared about how I felt, rather than keeping an eye on the time like a quack. Why would he care though? It's his job to ask me those questions. He's not paid to care. Is he? I really don't know.

One thing I know for sure is that he's the only person who has ever got me talking about Ben's death. I don't know how he did it! At least I know now to keep my guard up and not elaborate on what he already knows. I mean, how can I possibly explain to him my disjointed feelings when I simply don't understand them myself? Impossible!

I snap out of it quickly, knowing what will happen if I let myself fall into a sad state again. Immediately after my session with Blake, the gloomy feelings were so overwhelming that I ran straight to the kitchen to find myself a nice sharp knife. I was interrupted by the kitchen staff and was left unable to resort to my usual pain relief, though painful in itself.

Miserable, I plonk myself down on my bed. Tea tonight was very quiet—Jason and Rebecca weren't there for some reason. Blake and his wife, plus a few other staff have had dinner with us every night this week, which I guess is a nice gesture. I glance over at the camera that Blake gave me. Does he really expect me to use it? What would I say? That I'm okay and I can go home and I don't need to be here? I'll think of something, just not tonight—I'm exhausted. I crawl up towards the pillow and make it there just before I fall asleep.

I am awoken by a loud smashing noise coming from outside the building. I realise that I'm still fully clothed so I rush to the window to see what is going on. I wonder how long I've been asleep.

I look down at the beach and see Jason and Rebecca stumbling towards the shack. They look drunk! Rebecca is all over Jason, hugging him and using him to hold herself up. They're both laughing at something. At least someone is having some fun around here. That doesn't seem fair. I walk out onto the balcony, and see that Matthew is watching the event from his window. Within seconds, Blake comes running out with the security guard to see what is going on. Being just below me I am able to hear everything.

"What the hell is going on here?" Blake sounds furious. The two mischief-makers ignore him and continue laughing. "Well? Someone better start explaining or I'll get the police involved!"

Jason's face changes quickly from casual and blissful to furious.

"Don't you dare threaten me! I've had just about enough of that crap from you B—lake! Why don't you, and your little pussy friend here, go and find something useful to do! Take a chill pill and calm the hell down!"

Jason gets nose-to-nose with the security guard and gives him a hard shove sending him to the ground. Blake grabs him, puts him in an arm-hold and pushes him inside, treading over the broken vodka bottle that Jason had smashed. The security guard beckons the now silent Rebecca to follow so she does, with her head down.

A moment later, Blake announces over the P.A. system for us all to go to the hall for a meeting—immediately!

Matthew: Blake looks furious. He is pacing back and forth on the stage, obviously trying to figure out how to deal with the situation. I sure hope they don't get into too much trouble. All they were doing was blowing off some steam. Blake grabs the microphone, but slams it back down, deciding to use his powerful, booming voice for effect.

"I have called you all here, because although it is only two of you that have broken a very important rule, it is all of you who will be affected by it. In order for us to make some real progress here, we must work as a team. And if any part of that team fails, the rest of us will fail with them. That includes me." Blake's voice steadily calms down, although still very stern. I notice that all of the staff members are in the hall too. The chef seems to be hanging his head for some reason.

"Some of the rules explained to you on day one were—no drugs, alcohol, or violent behaviour—including vandalism. These rules have been put into place to protect you from the things that you have used in the past to express your anger and torment, or to hide or smother it. I understand all of this, I really do."

Blake looks serious, his eyes stare into the distance. He looks as though he is remembering something. I notice that Jason is glaring at him and Rebecca still has her head down.

"Now, anyone who breaks these rules is meant to be sent home immediately, no exceptions. Then you can face on your own whatever it is that you left behind."

Jason looks slightly pleased with this last comment.

"Whether that be drugs, crime, sex, violence, or even jail, there are no exceptions. But I personally believe it's a cop out. It's an easy way out. It's an easy way to avoid facing the real problems that got you all here. Much like drugs, alcohol, and even suicide can be the easy way out. What does it really solve? Nothing in the end. Deep inside each and every one of you there is a solution to the pain and anguish that engulfs you every day. We've just got to find it. But in order to find the answer, we must be a team. We must work together and respect one another."

Not bad, not bad. Similar to some of the sermons at the Catholic Church. Blake has got some real passion there. I can see it. But I don't know if he really understands the terrible things we've been through, that I've been through. How can he? That said, somehow I believe he really does care about us. I don't think the others realise that yet.

Rebecca: What the hell does he mean suicide is an easy way out? Does he realise what he just said? It's almost as if he knows what I just tried to do! And if he does, then does he know the reasons why I think about killing myself every day? No! So how dare he make a comment like that. If he's got a better solution, I'd like to see it. Because in my mind at the moment it's the only way out.

The only way.

And work as a team? Is he crazy? Tonight I realised that I do rely completely on drugs and alcohol to escape from reality. It is the only time I really feel safe from my dangerous thoughts. But who cares? Blake doesn't really care! He's a fake. He's too controlling.

He thinks he knows us. He thinks he knows me. He wouldn't have a clue.

"So, here's what we're going to do," Blake continues. "I didn't think it would be wise to do any team building exercises til you guys got to know each other well enough. But it looks like you already get along pretty well." He looks at me and Jason. "So tomorrow morning, early, we will begin with our first team challenge. Get some sleep, you'll need it!"

Oh great, a team challenge. I wonder if I can find another bottle of vodka. Or perhaps some pills of some sort. Maybe Matthew's pain medication. I've had enough of this. I want out, even more than I did before. I hate myself and I feel like crap.

"Hold it a minute!" Jason jumps to his feet before everyone moves out. "You can't just come in here with that shit rotten speech and expect us to *want* to be here and do your stupid challenge! Send me home! It's in the rules so why don't you do it?!"

I hate it when Jason gets angry—it scares me. I shift down a seat or two away from him.

"Jason." Blake looks at him gently. "We want to help you. We really do. We're giving you another chance here—seeing as that's what this place is all about. Why don't you just give us a chance too?"

Blake smiles and places a hand on Jason's shoulder.

I wince, expecting Jason to erupt in fists and cursing. Jason brushes Blake's hand off and opens his mouth to yell something but nothing comes out. He stares at Blake for a moment before storming out, kicking a few chairs over on the way. Blake walks over to me. Oh God, here comes the telling off. I shrink further into my chair.

"Rebecca." He places his hand on my shoulder. "Are you okay?"

I look up at him and nod. It is the first time I notice his gentle green eyes.

"It's okay. We're here to help you, not to punish or lecture you. See you tomorrow then?" He asks as if I have a choice before smiling and walking off towards the chef who is cowering in a corner.

Wow, what a shock! Here I am bracing myself for the drilling of a lifetime, the lecture of the century and the beating of the millennium and that's all he says? I still feel bad about what I did though. I am not used to having rules to stick to—rules that are there to keep me safe anyway. I suddenly become aware that the alcohol is still in my system and I begin to feel sick. Not sick physically because of the alcohol, but sick because I want the evil stuff out of my body. I never want to touch it again, and yet I crave it more than ever. I don't understand what's wrong with me! I hate this!

As I lie here on my bed looking out the window at the stars, I think about what happened earlier. I nearly died. My heart starts racing at the thought of it. That's the closest I've ever been to dying. Well I thought all those times taking an overdose of pills would've done the job, but somehow they didn't. And I especially thought my stash of heroin and other drug-filled syringes would've killed me for sure. I wonder why they didn't? I guess I'll never know. I don't know if I'm glad that they didn't work. And I don't know if I'm glad that Jason came to my rescue.

My hands tremble as I pick up the camera to look at the footage of Jason saving me. I can't believe he was there! I can't help but wonder what would have happened if he wasn't there. It would've been all over. I would've died. No more painful memories. No more terrifying flashbacks. No more life.

How did Jason find me? Was he following me and watching me the whole time? I wonder if he heard what I was saying. I don't usually pray but that time I did and every word is clear on the camera footage. I have no idea if God even exists or how to pray properly but it seems to have worked because I'm still here. Or was it all just luck? Who knows. What a strange and unfamiliar feeling—for the first time in my life I have a slither of gladness that I am alive.

Jason: I lounge around on the couch on the balcony and look out at the sea, glistening in the half-moon light. I still feel very relaxed from the booze and can feel myself drifting off. I don't mind though, it's a warm night so I'll just sleep out here. I wonder why Blake is so keen for us to give him a chance. Man he's a dickhead. I'd never give him anything. Not in a million years! I would never even talk to him in the street, unless it was to say something obscene or to mug him, so why would I give him a chance here?

He's dreaming.

Oh well. I'll pretend to enjoy this pointless activity tomorrow morning and then when the bus comes I'll be out of here. I'll even leave all my shit here so they can't tell I've gone. They'll just think I've gone for a long walk, like tonight. Man I'm good!

Ah what the hell. Why can't I sleep?

Something is bothering me.

I look towards the girls' rooms and wonder whether Rebecca is thinking about how I saved her and whether she still wants to kill herself. I hope she doesn't. She seems like a sweet girl, beneath it all. Way too bloody shy though. She's looking much better than day one—less sickly. I wonder what her real story is… I suddenly snap out of it and realise what I am thinking about. Why am I letting myself have these moments of softness? I truly don't care about her, do I? Maybe I do, maybe I don't, but it's not going to change anything. I'm still out of here tomorrow.

CHAPTER 6

~ Lost ~

Jason: Bloody hell, what is that racket? My sleep is broken by a very loud noise coming through the speaker system. It sounds like an air-horn or something.

"Wake up time!" Blake shouts joyfully through the speakers. "Breakfast is in twenty minutes!"

Are you serious? The sun only just went down! I'm still lying on the balcony couch and I realise there is a slight glow on the eastern horizon from the sun preparing to break through the darkness. I lie back down to grab five more minutes rest...

"Jason!" Blake is leaning over me. "Get up Jason, we're all ready to go!"

"But I only just..."

"Breakfast finished ten minutes ago. You'll have to grab some fruit or a muffin or something. Wear these." Blake passes me a pair of walking boots. "See you in the car." Blake disappears through the sliding door.

I jump up and pull a shirt on over my singlet. No time for a shower. I quickly change my socks and underwear, pull on my new shoes and run downstairs. Thank God this crap is almost over. I just need to get through today without drawing too much attention to myself and then I'll get out of here. I walk outside and see a big four-wheel-drive with the others already piled in. I grab a seat next to Felicity, who is staring at me as always. I roll my eyes and look out the window. The sun is breaking through. Blake passes us all eye masks and tells us to put them on—he doesn't want us to see where we're going. That's fine with me—a chance to get some more sleep. Even though the ride is bumpy along these dirt roads I fall asleep as soon as my head hits the head-rest.

Felicity: Why did Jason glare at me like that? I was only staring at him because he has his t-shirt on back-to-front! And he had the nerve to give me stink-eye thinking that I was checking him out or something! Ew, no thanks. Yes, he is kind of hot, but I just don't like angry guys—he shouts too often. I chuckle to myself after taking another peek at his lack of dressing ability.

I feel immensely better today compared to yesterday. My dark, crushing feelings have been replaced by a few more physical wounds, this time on my upper thighs to hide them from the others. Who would've known that the shattered glass from Jason's vodka bottle would come in handy. I can't explain why it helps but it just does. It had been a restless night up until the idea popped into my head. Even so, I only got a couple of hours rest so I place the mask back over my eyes and swiftly drift off to sleep.

I am awoken by sudden violent jerky movements of the four-wheel-drive. It feels as if we are on a roller coaster. We must be driving over some huge rocks or something because I am constantly being thrown from side-to-side, bouncing back and forth between Jason and Rebecca.

"Hold on tight!" I hear Blake's voice so I reach to grab something, but with nothing there I go flying upwards and can feel my stomach drop. Luckily for the seat belt or I would've gone through the roof!

"Where the hell are you taking us?" Jason questions Blake.

"You'll see! We're almost there," Blake answers and is held to his word because shortly after, the ride comes to a stop.

"We're here! Everybody out."

I take my blindfold off to see sunlight shining on thick, natural bushland. Wow, it looks amazing! I've never been camping before so I've never been this far bush. I can see the hilly, rocky track that we took, which obviously is rarely used because it is completely overgrown with low shrubs. Surrounding us are huge gumtrees and lots of other bright native plants and I can hear dozens of birds calling. Blake gathers us together.

"Today's exercise is about working as a team to achieve an objective. Your goal today is to use your common sense, natural ability, and your team-mates to find your way home. Of course, we are too far away from home to make you walk all that way, so we have given you a map with very minimal detail on how to get to a rendezvous point. It should take you no more than three or four hours. Oh and before I forget, the visiting schedule has been delayed three days to Tuesday okay? You will find out who your visitors are when they get here." Jason looks particularly upset at this news. Blake and the driver pull backpacks from the boot.

"Each of you has something in these backpacks that you will need to use to get home. There is also some food and water so make sure you stop for lunch."

"Blake." Matthew looks concerned. "I'm on crutches, so how do you expect me to walk for four hours in this bushland?"

"Yeah." Rebecca's eyes are wide with worry. "I've never really done any exercise in my life. I'm far too weak for this kind of thing."

"Matt." Blake looks sympathetic. "I saw you walk the entire length of the beach the other day without them. You'll be fine, so leave your crutches here. And Rebecca, you showed last night that you are fit enough to go gallivanting. If you guys are worried about anything or get into any trouble there is a two-way radio in each of the backpacks. Okay?"

Matthew and Rebecca both look unsure.

"Look guys," Blake says becoming a bit sterner. "This has to be done. Trust me, it's out here in the wilderness, with none of your usual worries or distractions that you'll make the most progress. Have confidence in yourself. I know you can do it."

"Yes sir!" Jason says sarcastically and does a mock salute as he pushes his way through. I roll my eyes. When will that boy grow up? I pick up the backpack and realise how heavy it is. Gosh, I can barely stand! It weighs much more than my school-bag, even with the large number of text-books I carry. I wonder what's in it to make it so heavy!

"Here's the map," Blake says and passes it to Rebecca. "Good luck, and let's see what you guys are made of!"

The four-wheel-drive takes off while Matthew and I huddle around Rebecca examining the map. Jason wanders off, starts picking up rocks and throwing them into the trees and at birds. He only just notices that his t-shirt is on backwards—this only makes him even more pissed off. What a loser! Anyway, the map consists of two checkpoints—one that says *Start* and another that says *Finish*. There isn't much in between except for a few landmarks to help guide us. The *Finish* looks like it is at the top of a hill or mountain. Great. I have to lug this stupid backpack all the way up a steep mountain! This sucks. It couldn't possibly get any worse.

Rebecca: Oh great, these guys probably think it's my fault that we're doing this because I got drunk last night. I bet they hate me. At least Jason was somewhat nice to me last night. He saved my life for goodness sake! I remember asking him random questions about anything. He answered most of them until I got to some more personal ones, such as his family and his tattoos. Those tattoos of his all have a special meaning. They are quite spectacular so I figured he'd be happy to explain them all. He told me briefly about most of them—they were gang-related and something to do with rank and allied crews. It was when I asked him about his *Vengeance* tattoo that he started to get defensive. I tried to change the subject by asking who the names were under the *R.I.P.* written in cursive across his left pec. This just made him so furious I thought he was gonna throw me off the cliff. He calmed back down when he realised I was just being a drunken little hoe. He'd be right to think that. It's all I am—just a dirty whore. He probably hates me just as much as the others do. Oh well, I don't care—I'm used to it.

Let's just get this over and done with.

Jason jogs back over once Blake's vehicle has disappeared.

"Let's head off and get this over with," he says, echoing my thoughts.

I pick up the backpack, which isn't very heavy at all, so I don't know what Felicity is complaining about. The boys don't seem to be complaining about theirs either. Maybe she's just weak. Jason makes a group decision to climb to the highest nearby ridge and see if we can spot the mountain we're supposed to end up at. Jason leads the way and sets a fairly brisk pace. Felicity already seems to be struggling with her backpack and falls behind very quickly. Why doesn't one of the boys help her with it or something? They don't seem to notice and just keep steaming ahead. Typical males. They disappear quickly through the thick scrub so I decide to wait for Felicity to catch up. She really is struggling! Not the sporty type I guess, not that I ever was. I don't think. I can't remember. I don't want to remember. I quickly block out any memories that try to rush back to me and grab Felicity by the hand. She looks shocked at this gesture, but smiles between her puffing and panting.

"Hey are you okay?" I ask her. "You look tired already! We've only been walking for fifteen minutes…"

"Yeah." She gasps for breath. "I've just…never carried anything this… this heavy before."

"That's okay, take your time." I pass her my water and she takes a long swig. "I'm sure the boys will wait for us. I think I can see the top of the hill now already. Are you okay to keep going?"

Felicity nods, so I pull her by the arm to help her up a rocky ledge. I can hear the boys yelling "Cooee!"

I shout back and follow the sounds of their voices, stumbling over rocks and fallen down logs, while also trying to help Felicity.

This is the first time since being here, besides when I was drunk, that I have felt completely at ease. It's a nice feeling for me. It's something I've never really felt before. It is possibly also because I don't feel like the only weakling anymore!

We finally manage to push our way through some thick shrubs and enter a clearing to find the boys. Jason is standing high up on a towering rock looking out across the valley. Matthew is leaning against another rock having a drink of water, ignoring the view. Felicity drops her bag immediately and flops down onto a mossy patch, still trying to catch her breath. I notice that she is rubbing her back. Gee, she really must be weak!

"I can see the mountain," Jason calls out and points in its general direction.

I rush over, stopping just before the ledge and look out over the valley.

Oh my God.

It is beautiful. I have never seen anything like it. I may even like this view better than the beach back at camp! The valley stretches far and dips steeply, covered completely in a carpet of green trees, before sloping upwards into a peak—the mountain we must reach. Well it's really more of large hill. I've never seen a real mountain before, but I always imagined them to be massive, towering, snow-covered peaks, that disappear into the clouds. This one sure looks steep, but doesn't look all that tall—from here anyway. In the middle of the valley there is a lake, or river of some sort. It sure looks pretty from up here! God only knows where we are though.

Jason grabs the map from me and I realise he had climbed down from his tower. He points to the river drawn on the map and then at the actual river.

"We've just gotta go straight down there," he begins, a bit of excitement in his voice. "We'll find a way across the river, which will make it about lunch time, then make for that mountain." He semi-smiles at me, but walks off before noticing me smile back.

Matthew: I look at Jason and cannot figure out whether he is being genuine or not. He seems to want to get this activity done as quick as possible. I tried to talk to him just before but he ignored me and climbed that rock. At least he hasn't tried to beat me up again! I better not get on his nerves though, with no-one else out here to stop him if he does decide to beat up on me. I'll just play it cool. I've learnt to stay in the shadows when there's danger around so this should be easy. But

I've never been forced to walk this close to danger—since escaping my homeland anyway. And there I could run and hide if I wanted to. I feel as if Jason is like one of those unexploded bombs near my home village—peaceful looking while just sitting there but everyone keeps their distance never knowing when it might go off.

I notice that Jason is over at Felicity asking her something. She points to her backpack and he reaches over to it and lifts it up. Then he opens it and pulls out the contents—there's a lunchbox with some food, a huge bottle of water, a first-aid kit, sunscreen, and a harness. After he places those things on the ground he tips the backpack upside down and out tumble four huge rocks. I decide to wander over to see what they are, as Rebecca has also joined them. When I reach them, I notice that the rocks are actually bricks, and pretty big ones too!

"So that's why you were struggling so much," Rebecca says and smiles at her. "We might as well leave them here then. Blake is tricky!"

Felicity nods her head. "See, I'm not weak! You should've tried carrying that thing!"

"Yeah check out these guns," Jason says and wraps a couple of his fingers around Felicity's petite biceps. They all laugh, and I try to join in but feel kind of left out. Nothing ever changes I guess. Everyone has their little groups and I guess there's no room anywhere for the homeless black guy. Oh well, I'm used to it. I feel kind of bad for not checking on Felicity while she was struggling with the backpack. I cannot believe that Jason was the one to help her out. Jason, I don't get this guy. He's got more mood swings than I can count. I snap out of it when Felicity jumps up and grabs me by the hand, dragging me away from the other two.

"Come and show me this view!" She holds my hand until we're on the highest point and we both say "wow!" at the same time. I have seen some spectacular views in my journeys, but none as breathtaking as this. It is almost like a beautiful painting—I even reach out to see if it's real.

Then, as suddenly as she came, Felicity climbs back down to collect her backpack, urging us all to keep going.

Jason: "Why would Blake put bricks in your backpack?" I ask Felicity as I help her climb down some rocks.

"I dunno. Who cares? Why would he dump us in the middle of nowhere anyhow? At least I can actually attempt to keep up with you guys now!" She laughs and I laugh back. I have a good feeling about completing this task—even if I do have to work as a team with these losers. I figure that pretending to be nice will make them less suspicious about my plans to escape, plus it'll keep Blake off my back til then. I used to be a nice guy so I know how to do it when I want to, even if it does make me sick.

We continue on through the dense bushland, heading down towards the river. I remembered that Felicity also had a harness in her backpack and I begin to dread the thought of having to rock-climb or something. I mean, *I* am capable of doing anything that Blake's got in store for us, but I'm a bit worried about the rest of the group. I guess that's where working as a team will come in. Gee, I can't wait.

We finally manage to make it to the river—it only took us an hour, and it looks like we're half-way so we're going to make good time. That's excellent news—I can't wait to get out of here and back home where I belong. There is a nice patch of grass next to the river, which we sit ourselves on to have lunch. As we open our lunchboxes we notice that each of us has an envelope with our names on it. Bloody hell, what is this going to be? I screw my face up as I open mine, while shovelling a sandwich into my mouth. It reads:

> "Jason,
> Well done on making it this far. Hopefully you're heading in the right direction and we'll see you soon! Don't give up on your friends here. They will need you more than you know it. You'll see. Trust me. And remember—never let pride take the place of humility.
> Blake."

Are you kidding me? What a pointless letter! Why would he even bother? I'll never trust him. And I'll especially never help these guys, unless I get something out of it, which I plan to do. I screw mine up and throw it into the dirt.

The others are still reading their letters so I move onto my second sandwich. Man, I'm hungry! Oh yeah, that's right, I missed out on breakfast! I might have to steal some of the girls' food.

"Oh no." Felicity looks very worried. "We have a slight problem here guys." She passes Rebecca the note. "It says that the bricks in my backpack must be carried all of the way to the finish in order to be successful. If they are not, then we will have to start again from the beginning!"

"Bloody Blake," I declare loudly, suddenly feeling my usual rage bubbling up. "That stupid tosspot! I knew there was a reason those bricks were in there. He wanted us to share the load. Great, I guess I'll have to go back and get them." I get up and start to walk off in a huff, imagining myself punching Blake's nose in.

"I'll come with you," I hear Matthew's voice, which makes me scowl. "I'll help you Jason."

I turn my head slightly to see Matthew walking towards me after tipping the contents of his backpack onto the ground and placing his own note in his pocket. My first instinct is to say no, or tell him to piss off. Part of me wants to hit him again, but deep down I know I shouldn't—for now. But why shouldn't I? He's just a scumbag, right? Yeah, I still want to smash this bloke. Nobody here would be able to stop me. It'd be an unfair fight though. I normally don't bash people weaker than me—unless there's a whole group, or I've got a good reason. Maybe I'll wait til we're well away from the girls so they can't hear.

Oh I don't know anymore. At least if he comes, I won't have to carry them all by myself. And besides, if I said no he'd probably run off with the girls or something and leave me behind.

"Alright," I say to him, half-scowling. "Let's go then. Try to keep up. And no talkin'. I'm not interested in what you've got to say. We'll be back soon girls."

I start jogging at a swift pace back up the hill, and I can hear Matthew's footsteps right behind me. I slow down a bit when my chest starts to hurt because I am breathing so deeply. Maybe it's too early to start running again. Matthew overtakes me, striding ahead quickly.

This sparks something inside me that makes me forget my intense pain and I begin running as fast as I can possibly go over such rough terrain, ducking and weaving to avoid being hit by low-hanging branches. I pass Matthew and take the lead again. That's the last time I'll let *him* get in front. I keep this pace up pretty much all the way to the top, apart from a few treacherous spots where we had to slow down.

I climb up the cliff, which leads to the clearing where we left the bricks. I notice that Matthew, the persistent little bugger is struggling to climb up the cliff but I pretend not to see. He's the one who chose to come, so he can help himself! And I didn't force him to climb that cliff—he could've waited. I pick up one of the bricks and notice that it has my name on it. What is going on here? I pick up the other bricks and, sure enough, everyone's name is on one of them. Well, I wish we'd seen that before! Matthew finally makes it up the cliff and chucks me the backpack.

"Phew, that was tough," Matthew says, trying to catch his breath. I nod and place the bricks in the backpack. Man, he is weak. I should push him off the cliff. It'd be too easy and would look like he tripped.

"That's it, let's go back," I say and begin to walk off. "We'll take it in turns carryin' this thing. You go down the cliff first and I'll lower it to you."

Matthew nods and jumps into action. He is much quicker climbing down than up. I pass him the backpack by using one of the straps to lower it down the initial steep part before letting it slide the rest of the way. I breeze down the cliff, grab the backpack and begin to jog off, with Matthew in hot pursuit. This is too easy; I didn't need this idiot to come with me. I should just tie him up and leave him here. I smirk at the idea and decide to pick up the pace.

Matthew: Hmm, Jason still hates me doesn't he? Why does he hate me so much? I haven't done anything to him! He won't even look me in the eye or talk to me. He just left me struggling up that cliff, even though he knows my arms are still wounded. He's just a skinhead thug. He won't change, so why does *he* deserve a second chance? I'm the one who hasn't even had a chance to live a proper, decent life, and not by choice. I don't know why he's so angry. If only he knew what I've been through. I guess I'll just have to show him my video and then he might listen, but I doubt it. He only cares about himself. Selfish prick.

All of a sudden, Jason trips over a log and falls heavily onto the rocky ground, the bag crashing down onto his back. He lies there stunned for a moment, then begins cursing and shouting every swear word under the sun.

Without hesitation I walk over and reach down to help him but he pushes my hand away.

"I'll be okay," he mumbles. He pulls up his pant leg to reveal a fairly deep gash in his shin, which is bleeding heavily. Once more, Jason begins swearing his head off. While he is cursing, I take my singlet off and tear it lengthways a few times to make a bandage.

"Let me put this on." I beckon to Jason to let me help him. "It'll help stop the bleeding."

Jason starts to push my hand away again but finally gives in. I wrap the make-shift bandage around his wound and partially further up and down the leg before tying it off.

"How does that feel?" I ask him. "Let me know if it's too tight okay?"

"It's fine." Jason nods and looks down at the bandage. He doesn't even thank me, but I didn't expect he would, even though it would be nice. I guess he'll never warm to me. I'm glad I don't expect much of people anymore, or I would constantly be disappointed.

Jason slowly gets up and attempts to walk but winces in pain.

"I think I sprained an ankle too," he says, followed by a few more cursed words.

"Bummer," I say, trying to look sincere. "I'll carry the backpack rest of the way okay?"

He nods and drops the backpack for me to pick up. We walk off slowly but Jason's legs give way.

"It's too painful," Jason says, clearly very angry. "My ankle…"

Before the ticking-time-bomb Jason explodes I find an appropriately sized branch and grab it for him to use as a walking-stick. I pass it to him and smile.

"Use this champ. It'll help take the weight off your leg. If not, you can lean on me and hop the rest of the way!"

Jason looks a bit stunned, and his normal icy gaze melts for a fraction of a second.

"Thanks mate." Jason sounds uneasy in his reply but at least he's trying.

"No worries, anytime," I tell him, and give him a quick, cautious pat on his back. I hope I'm not pushing my luck here. I must remember that this is the guy who beat me up on the second day! Hmmm, forgive and forget I guess. That's easier said than done, but I'll do my best. Besides, it's not worth holding grudges, especially when you're alone with the person! We're in this together.

I shake my head and follow Jason, keeping an eye out just in case he topples over again.

✳ ✳ ✳ ✳

"They should be having their lunch right about now Tim," Blake says to his driver as they arrive at their destination. Tim nods and grabs their own lunch to eat, while Blake sets up some chairs for the two of them to sit in and wait for the group to arrive.

"Do you think they'll make it?" Tim asks Blake, looking a bit sceptical.

Blake looks out across the valley from the mountainside.

"I just hope they choose the right mountain!" Blake says jokingly and they laugh. "Nah, they'll be fine. Once they cross the river and make it to the top of Hell's Stairway they'll be fine."

"Oh, so you did decide to make them go that way? I thought you said that would be too difficult..."

Blake sighs and nods. "Well there are other ways to get here, but I think they'll choose that way. Otherwise they'll have to walk all the way around to the other side of the mountain to reach the four-wheel-drive track and take that way up." Blake leans back in his chair thoughtfully. "We'll see... We'll see."

CHAPTER 7

~ Unite or Fight ~

Felicity: I look intently at Rebecca while she eats. I wonder why she isn't talking to me. She said a few words earlier today but not much and now she's back to her old, quiet self—hiding away in her shell. Maybe she has a problem with me or something. She seemed to be getting along quite nicely with Jason last night! I don't know why I haven't been getting much attention—I'm usually the popular one! I'm not used to being ignored. I suddenly feel my mood begin to change and the whole world starts to become dim again. I quickly try to think of something nice to distract me before I lose myself in the dark abyss of my mind. I watch some birds playing in the water and chasing insects through the air. I listen to the breeze blowing gently through the trees and enjoy the warmth of the sun's rays on my bare, tanned shoulders.

Phew, that was close. I can't let myself become weak like that again.

I look back over at Rebecca who is now staring strangely at me.

"You're bleeding," she calls out and moves to get up.

I look down and notice that some blood has seeped through my shorts.

Oh shit.

I quickly jump off my rock and run to the safety of the shrubs. Oh God, what will she think now? I remove my shorts but then realise that the first aid kit is still in my backpack. I begin to pull my shorts back up and am suddenly interrupted by a rustling noise.

"Are you okay?" Rebecca calls as she pushes her way through the thick bushes.

How embarrassing.

"Yes thanks," I say abruptly to try and deter her.

"Here," she says and passes me the first aid kit.

I freeze like a stunned mullet. I realise that my shorts aren't quite all the way up and Rebecca can see my freshly de-scabbed wounds—the walking and climbing must've done it. What was I thinking? I'm usually much better at hiding my shameful self-harm wounds.

"It's okay Felicity." Rebecca interrupts my state of shock. "I won't tell the others."

I watch her as she pulls out a dressing and a roller bandage from the first aid kit.

"Hold this on your graze," she says gently as she passes me the dressing. I've never seen a "graze" this long, parallel and purposeful before but I think Rebecca meant to use that word instead of "cut". She wraps the bandage around my leg so it's tight enough to stem the seeping wounds.

"Why are you doing this?"

"I dunno." Rebecca shrugs. "I've seen worse."

I watch her as she hurries back to her lunch. I don't know if I trust Rebecca with this deeply personal secret of mine but somehow, I don't know how, I think she understands.

I wonder where the boys are. They've been gone for a while. I want to get out of here before I lose my mind. I've been trying so hard to be strong—at least to try and look like I'm okay. It won't last long though, these defences of mine. I'll lose it, sooner or later. I always do.

Finally I see the guys stumble out into the clearing—Jason is using Matthew's shoulder to lean on and is hopping on one foot. It's an impossible sight, but certainly one to see.

"Hey guys." I get up and walk towards them. "What happened?"

Jason ignores me and limps over to a rock to sit down. I look at Matthew for an answer.

"He had a fall," Matthew begins, smiling. "It was spectacular! What a stuntman!"

Whoa, one quick trip together and now they're mates? What's going on here? I thought Jason wanted to kill Matthew!

"So you carried him back then?" I ask with a smirk.

Matthew shrugs and nods. "Yeah well he wanted to keep running, but no-one should even be walking with an injury that bad."

Jason looks over at us and I can tell he wants to say something, most likely rude, but holds back. Matthew grabs the first-aid kit and walks over to Jason. After taking off the make-shift bandage, Matthew puts a proper dressing on it and bandages up Jason's sprained ankle.

"Where'd ya learn how to do all this?" Jason asks, looking a bit bothered.

Matthew doesn't look up from what he is doing and simply says—"On the streets."

On the streets?

It was then that I realised that Matthew is homeless. I had no idea. Jason looks just as astounded as I am.

Rebecca: I can't stand this much longer. Felicity glared at me pretty much the whole time the boys were gone and now that they're back she can't stop giving them all her attention! Look at her—all over them, pretending to be concerned. What a flirt. Slut. She doesn't know what men are really like. If only she'd actually try to talk to me properly we might get along. She didn't even thank me for helping her with her cuts. I don't know why I bothered to help her. It was difficult enough, knowing full well it would bring back memories of the girls back at the brothel. There were a few cutters there, and quite often I would be the one to fix them up. Why on earth would Felicity need to do such a thing though? She's the luckiest girl I've ever met.

She's tall, thin, smart, sexy and rich. What more could she possibly want? She must really be messed up in the head. How pathetic.

Oh crap. Her neck.

That's why she has that cut on her neck. How could I not have seen that? I'm so stupid. She mentioned that she got mugged and someone slit her throat, and it never even clicked that she had done it herself. Holy shit, maybe she is for real. It still doesn't mean she can ignore me, bitch.

I know that I need to talk to someone, but I just can't. The anger and resentment are still strong, but I want to bury all of my painful memories for good. I haven't been sober for this long in ages and it's becoming hard to stop the flashbacks. Especially when things like this stir up memories—I'll let my mind relax too much and drop my barriers and suddenly it's filled with terrifying images that are nearly impossible to remove. I have been waking up in cold sweats because of nightmares and I don't have the guts to seek any help. I just cower in a ball til I'm too exhausted to stay awake. But I can't do this anymore. It's killing me inside. I want to start again and make new and better memories without ever mentioning the terrifying ones again. I don't have to tell these guys anything, so I won't. They probably wouldn't believe me anyway.

"Hey Rebecca." Jason's voice startles me. "We're ready to leave now if you are."

I nod at him and try to say thanks but only a squeak comes out. I feel my face go hot. I wonder what he thinks of me.

We pick up our packs and start walking, Jason is still limping but he is using a big stick to help him along. The guys are carrying two stones each in their backpacks, with us girls carrying the lighter stuff. I can hear Felicity moaning about something.

"Oh great," she says. "The rest of the trip is uphill, and look how big that mountain is!"

I look up, and notice how big the hill actually looks from down here.

"Well at least you're not carrying these stones!" Matthew jokes.

"Yeah I think I carried them far enough earlier," she replies dryly.

Matthew has cheered up a lot and I can tell he's trying to either unite the group or just make some friends, or both.

God this is so hard. I've never done exercise like this before. We've been going for at least an hour since lunch and every time I look up, the mountain just seems to get bigger! I'm so exhausted that I can't even enjoy the beauty of this place, even though it is the first time I've been somewhere like this. We stop next to a huge towering cliff and Jason examines the map.

"This is the spot." He points towards the cliff and my heart sinks. "We have to climb this."

His statement confirms my fear. There is no way that I'm climbing this cliff! I'll never make it to the top! Thank goodness Felicity looks just as terrified as I am.

"We can't climb that thing!" Felicity objects. "How do you expect us to climb that Jason? Especially with our backpacks!"

I totally agree with Felicity but decide to hang back and let them argue. The cliff has an almost vertical slope to it, and lots of rocks jutting out of it, which would make it easier to climb if you were experienced enough, which I certainly am not. I don't think it would matter so much if it wasn't as high. We could just find a way around. But this cliff takes up half the hillside with its enormous height and length. We'd probably have to walk for ages to get around to the other side and find an easier way up—if there even is an easier way! I just hope Blake knew what he was doing when he organised this little trip. Jason asks us to pull out our harnesses and put them on. He doesn't even bother to put his own harness on and walks over to examine the cliff. Felicity refuses to budge. She plonks herself down onto the ground and sits there like a spoiled brat trying to get her own way.

"You'll have to carry me up then," she sulks, crossing her arms.

I decide to join her. She looks at me, first in disbelief, then unsure, then relieved that someone else agrees with her. She even mouths "Thank you."

Jason: Bloody hell, girls can be so damn frustrating and stubborn sometimes! This cliff doesn't look too hard to climb. Don't get me wrong—it is very tall, but it doesn't look very complicated to climb. It has staggered offset rocks jutting out, almost like huge steps. And I *will* carry the girls up there if I have to! I just want to get the hell out of here!

"Come on girls," I plead with them, hiding my irritation as best I can. "Look, there's no obvious way around this. Blake clearly wants us to work as a team and get up this thing. If we can do that then maybe we can finally go home. And I promise you'll never have to see me again! But watch, I have a sprained ankle and I can still climb it easily!"

I pull myself up and climb for a few metres to prove how easy it is, even though the throbbing pain in my leg and ankle is almost unbearable. I suck it up—I've had worse injuries before.

"I'm still not doing it!" Felicity shouts as I continue to climb. I shake my head and concentrate on finding some good hand holds, as I am trying not to put too much pressure on my injured leg. I figure that if I can make it to the top, set up the rope for their harnesses, I'll be able to help them up. If not, then we'll get on the radio and tell Blake we're stuck. But that's the last resort—I don't want to be seen as a failure, especially in front of *these* fools.

I decide not to look down until I reach the top, as I must concentrate on not slipping. Imagine I fell—that would hurt! Not that anyone would care though. Hey, what am I saying?! These guys probably wouldn't care, but my gang needs me back at home. They would definitely miss me, wouldn't they? I shake my head to clear my mind of these conflicting thoughts and continue to climb.

I finally make it half-way and decide to rest myself on a small ledge. I hear Felicity ranting and raving about something, and she even yells mockingly up at me to ask if I've given up! Is she crazy? I should push a boulder off onto their stupid little heads. I realise how terrible that sounds as soon as I think it and decide to continue climbing. This time I decide not to look up or down—I'll just concentrate on where I'm at, when I get there. I also figure out a new technique to help swing myself up without putting any pressure on my sore foot. This works well, as soon after I make it to the top. I sit for a bit to relax, and think about how funny it would be if I just left them down there and ran off. I roll my eyes and sigh, and then tie the rope securely to a tree, loop it around another tree to act as a pulley, and throw the remainder down the cliff to the others. I guess I may as well do the right thing.

"I'll pull the bags up first," I call down to the others. I can only see them if I lean forward, using the rope for safety, as there are a couple of huge boulders blocking the view. Matthew ties one bag at a time and I pull them all up with ease. I yell out to Matthew to let the girls go first, and he connects the rope to their harness. Rebecca goes first, as Felicity is still sulking. God, she's a spoiled little brat! How friggen annoying. Argh, I could strangle her sometimes!

Rebecca takes twice as long as I did, even with me helping her by pulling her up the difficult sections. She collapses on the ground next to me, red in the face from all that exertion.

"Phew, I made it," Rebecca murmurs and quickly looks the other way.

"Yeah, now let's see if Felicity can do it," I mutter sarcastically, as I drop the rope back down.

I can hear Matthew and Felicity arguing for a moment, but can't make out what they're saying. Finally I feel a tug on the rope as she begins to climb. I lean back and take some of her weight, while pulling up the slack. Rebecca helps by pulling the rope tight around the first tree to make it safer in case Felicity falls. She takes just as long as Rebecca, and when I can hear her near the top I reach over to grab her hand and see that it is actually Matthew! As I clasp his hand I contemplate letting go, but I quickly pull him up before I get a chance to let him fall.

"She wouldn't budge, Jason," he says between breaths. "I tried, but she's too stubborn."

I help Matthew up and he sits by Rebecca after thanking me.

"I'll go down and carry the little brat up then," I say as I attach the rope to my harness. I use the rope and harness to abseil down and reach the bottom in no time. As I drop down the last section I land hard on my sore ankle causing an intense pain to shoot up my leg. I curse at the top of my lungs and it echoes throughout the valley.

"You guys alright down there?" Matthew leans out to check on us. I flip him the bird. My aggravation is getting difficult to contain.

Felicity is sitting in the same spot as when I left. She looks like she is crying, and once I get closer to her I realise that she is.

"Come on then, we've got to climb this thing," I say, trying hard to cover up my frustration. She begins to object, but then bursts out into tears. I sit next to her and reluctantly put an arm around her.

"What is it Felicity? What's wrong?"

She sobs for a moment longer before looking up at me.

"I'm afraid of heights," she blubbers. "I can't climb that cliff Jason, I just can't."

I roll my eyes and sigh. I think about giving up. Not after coming all this way though.

"Yes you can." I look at her, this time with some sincerity to hide my impatience. "And you will. I'll help you. The rope will be tied to you, with Matthew and Rebecca helping from the top. I'll follow you and help you up the difficult parts okay?"

"Okay," she says and wipes her eyes on her sleeve. "But I'm scared."

"I know," I say and give her a quick hug. "You'll be fine. Even the other two got up there, and I did with a sore leg. Once you're up there, you'll wanna climb back down and do it again!"

She laughs uneasily and smiles. "Okay, let's do it then."

I grin back and tie the rope to her harness. She takes one last deep breath and attacks the climb with all the strength left in her. I follow closely behind, giving her encouragement and guiding her up the difficult sections. At one point where she is struggling I reach up to give her a boost by gripping her lower thighs. My hands accidentally shift her shorts up and I notice some bandages wrapped around her thighs, with spots of red seeping through. Felicity looks down at me, her eyes wide with fear. I don't know what to say.

"Are you okay? When did you hurt yourself?"

"I didn't," she says defensively and jumps back into action.

Gee, I didn't know she had even injured herself. Maybe it happened before she was brought to this place, but whatever happened I hope she's okay. It's an unusual spot for an injury. A sick feeling rises up in my stomach when I realise the only other place I've seen wounds in that area—when a close female friend was sexually abused. They cut her thighs as well to make a point. I shake my head and look up to see that Felicity is quickly getting the hang of it and races up the cliff, leaving me in her dust! Once I finally make it up again I can see her bragging about her efforts to the others.

"See, I don't know what you were worried about!" I declare, still a little surprised at her courageous effort. "You've done this before, haven't you?"

"No way," she says, triumphantly proud of herself. "I just wanted to get up as quickly as possible! I was too scared to look down."

She laughs and everyone else does too. I can sense a bit of uncertainty when Felicity looks at me. I won't ask her about her bandaged legs, it's obvious she doesn't want to talk about it. Not yet anyway.

Maybe she isn't such a spoiled brat after all. Perhaps she was just scared and needed that little extra push to climb the cliff. Maybe Blake was right, and I feel a bit better about being here—I'm actually beginning to enjoy myself, funnily enough. It reminds me of the good old days, playing with my brothers and sister. But I still don't know, and I'm definitely not changing my mind about leaving, no matter what—even if I have to wait longer now.

Matthew: As we continue walking, I still can't believe how good this trip has been. It feels like a holiday, an adventure. It reminds me of when my family had to escape our country, trekking through the jungles to get to the coast—although this bushland feels a lot safer! I sigh about the memories of my family and wonder if I'll ever see them again. I wonder where they live these days, and if my brothers were able to go to school. I wonder if my dad found a job and if they were living happy lives. I wonder why they've fallen off the radar and haven't tried to contact me. I wonder if they even searched for me when we were separated.

"Matthew." Felicity breaks through my thoughts. "Thanks for helping to pull me up. Just knowing that you weren't going to let go gave me the courage to climb all that way."

"How'd you know I wouldn't let go?" I tease her, and give her one of my big, cheesy grins that haven't been seen in a long time.

"Oh I just knew." She smiles at me, and I notice her beautiful blue eyes. She grabs onto my hand, sending a shiver up my spine, and I know that I've found a lifelong friend. The walk up this mountain trail is much easier than through the bushland in the valley, as there are less trees and shrubs. It isn't long before we reach the top, which plateaus off rapidly revealing a large clearing surrounded by trees. In the middle of the clearing is the four-wheel-drive, with Blake sitting there waiting for us. As soon as he spots us he runs towards us clapping and cheering, with the driver following suit. Felicity drops her bag and runs to give him a big hug. She really has loosened up! He groups us together and takes a photo of us, with Jason groaning about getting his picture taken. He manages to look away in each photo though, which annoys Blake a bit.

"Nice work everyone!" Blake looks very pleased indeed. "I'm very impressed. You took longer than I thought, but I guess I underestimated the difficulty of that cliff!"

I glance at Jason knowing that the cliff wasn't the only reason we took so long. I get the feeling Blake somehow knew as well. Blake walks around and shakes everyone's hand. I walk up and shake Jason's hand too, and he nods, hopefully in respect.

"Now, have you still got those slabs I placed in one of the backpacks?" Blake asks this with a look of excitement glowing on his face.

"Yes!" Felicity exclaims. "They were in *my* backpack! Thanks a lot Blake!"

They laugh, and then Jason and I take the bricks out of our bags.

"Okay good." Blake picks up one of the bricks. "These bricks represent that each one of you passed this vital part of your journey with flying colours. You probably don't think much of this hike, but trust me, the healing has begun. We're going to make a special wall with your bricks, and every other group that follows. Seeing you are the first group in this new program, you get to decide where this wall will be built!" Blake gestures at the entire clearing and declares, "Take your pick!"

We all stand there in silence, waiting for someone else to make the choice. Finally Jason steps forward and points over towards a nice green patch of grass, surrounded by some bright flowering shrubs.

"How about over there?" Jason says, and picks up his brick. We all walk over to the spot and place our bricks on the ground, arranging them nicely. We stand there and admire the symbol of our achievement—the first one as a group.

"Fantastic job everyone," Blake says. "I'm very proud of you all. I know you worked well as a team, and this is just the beginning. So, who wants to go home for some tea?"

We all cheer and run back to the four-wheel-drive. To my surprise, but possibly just by chance, Jason sits next to me.

CHAPTER 8

~ *Opening Up* ~

Rebecca: I wish I wasn't here right now. I feel like crying, I feel like runnin' down the beach and crawling into a hole. Most of all, I feel like hugging Matthew right now, just like Felicity is. He showed the group what he has done of his video so far. It is only short and he stops abruptly when he gets upset but I think it says enough. I can't believe he is a refugee. His country must really have been bad for his family to be desperate enough to escape. I wonder how they did manage to escape—maybe he'll keep filming and explain the rest. I hope he does.

Watching him talk with such emotion really got to me. I really wish I could burst into tears but instead I'm hiding here away from the others. Even Jason gives Matthew a pat on the back and shows some respect. Blake decides to take the group down to the beach for a discussion. Thank goodness he took the attention away from Matt, for now—I just felt way too left out and self-conscious. Maybe I'll give him a hug later.

We walk until we find a perfect spot on the beach. Being in such a picturesque place makes me feel better already.

"Thank you for showing us that Matthew." Blake smiles widely. "And I'm really impressed by the way you all responded to him."

Not me. I stare at the sand and hope he doesn't ask me anything.

"Does anyone have anything to say about what Matthew said?"

Nobody answers—great, now he'll probably go around the group asking everyone. I wish I wasn't here. I wonder if I can bury my head in the sand.

"It's okay," Matthew speaks up. "I think I'm ready to tell the rest of the story now, if that's okay with you Blake?"

"Absolutely, go for it."

Matthew shifts uncomfortably and stares out to sea while he gathers his thoughts.

"Um, I'll continue with what happened when we escaped. We had to wait in our hiding spot for two days before the soldiers stopped looking for people in the town. We snuck out carefully and checked all our neighbours' homes. They were either empty or we found, ah, the dead bodies of our friends and people we knew. We grabbed what we could, which wasn't much because the houses had been looted, and began our journey through the jungle. This jungle was a lot more dangerous than the one we went through the other day, if you can even call that a jungle! This one had a lot of wild animals, snakes and spiders, and of course, the enemy soldiers. We even had to cross a raging river and followed that for a few days east. After spending weeks trekking through hard terrain, we let our guard down one night and a stray soldier looking for a place to do a piss stumbled upon us and started shouting to his comrades. I woke up just as my dad killed him."

Matthew's eyes are wide and fixed on one spot on the ground.

"It was either him or us my dad told me. We had to leave straight away, leaving everything behind, with the soldier's friends in hot pursuit, bullets flying past us close, too close. My dad had to carry my youngest brother most of the way, which slowed us down. We ate whatever we could find—small animals, raw fish, bird eggs, plant roots. After about another week we stumbled across a road and managed to flag down a truck. Soon after, my father realised we had entered a neighbouring country that borders the ocean.

We were hungry, thirsty, exhausted and frightened, with nowhere to go. We had no money, so my dad went into the local market to see what he could steal for us to eat. He came back with nothing, but told us that he had met a nice woman who invited us to stay at her house, where she would cook us a meal. It was the best meal I've ever had, even though it wasn't much. But after weeks of eating shit-all it was a feast. We all fell asleep pretty much straight after."

I look around the group and notice that everyone is completely wrapped up in Matthew's story. I'm also very interested, but sad at the same time. I wish I was brave enough to tell my own story. I snap out of it and concentrate on Matt.

"I woke up the next morning to find my dad missing," he continues. "I looked around the woman's small cottage and couldn't find her either. My brothers and mother were still sleeping. Suddenly my dad ran inside screaming for the others to get up because we had to go. I asked why but he just kept telling me to hurry up. He had a big basket of food and some other things, so I figured he must've stolen them and had been caught or something. I was wrong. It turned out that the woman knew we were trying to escape and went to turn us in for a reward. My dad was running away from the soldiers.

Anyway, we ran down to the wharf and managed to steal a small boat, which we used to get away. The soldiers fired upon us, my dad got hit, luckily only his arm. We sailed for almost two weeks in that dinghy. Once we had run out of food and water, and were unable to catch any more fish, my dad gave up. He pulled out his gun and said—'This is for the best.' Without hesitation he pulled the trigger…"

Felicity gasps and I realise that I did too, my hand rushing up to my mouth.

"It was okay though, the gun didn't go off. Something was wrong with it, but I grabbed it off him and threw it into the water. After yelling at him he calmed down and apologised. Anyway, it felt like an age—starving, thirsty, sun-burnt and we prepared ourselves for the worse. A slow painful death. But it was actually not long after, a bigger fishing boat came by and picked us up. They asked where we were heading and my dad said—'Anywhere', so they took us on another three week long journey, where finally we got to see dry land again. We ran around cheering and hugging one another, thanking God that we made it here. We thought that our lives were saved and everything would be better, until the first town we stayed in made us wish we were back home. Well almost.

My dad managed to get a job at a bar, cleaning and all that business for a few months, and he thought he was doing my mother a favour by getting her a job too. But the owner of the bar, after finding out we were refugees, forced her to work in his brothel for no extra money, or he'd turn us in to the authorities."

Oh God, my heart begins to race a million miles an hour, and my eyes begin to well up. I hate hearing that evil word, *brothel*, but I also cannot believe what I am actually listening to. I know how Matthew feels, in a way, but I don't know what to do about it. My stomach feels sick with despair.

"My dad, who is ready to kill the guy, decides that we need to escape again. We make a run for it one night and stow away on a train that was to take us all the way across the country to Sydney."

Matthew pauses, looking across the sea again. He clears his throat and looks very emotional. Felicity grabs his hand to comfort him.

"The last time I saw my family was when I woke up to my dad yelling for us to jump off the train. He was hysterical, saying that the security guards had found us and that we had to bail off the train or we would be arrested and probably deported. I grabbed my bag and readied myself to jump. I remember looking back to see my family getting grabbed by the security guards, my dad still telling me to jump. So I did. I landed on a grassy embankment, breaking my wrist. So yeah, that's pretty much how I got here."

Everyone looks just as amazed as I feel. Matthew has seen the world, while all I know is the four walls of the prison that kept me captive for so long. If I ever have to go back there I'll die.

"But what happened after?" Felicity asked, looking puzzled. "Surely that's not the end of the story. You were only ten or eleven years-old when all of this happened, right?"

"Well, yes you're right," he hesitates. "This was the beginning of my homeless life. I have many more stories about living on the streets, in parklands, in half-built houses—but I'll save all that for later. I'll have to go into more detail, maybe when I continue my video. But yes, it was extremely hard for me, as you can only imagine, because I was so young. I still have terrifying flashbacks every single day."

Matthew looks at us for the first time.

"The only thing that has kept me going all this time is the hope of being able to see my family once again."

I feel a warm, wet tear rolling down my cheek—my first honest, heartfelt tear in years.

Jason: Oh man, I had no idea what this kid has been through. I still probably don't even know the half of it, but from what I've heard so far it's pretty crazy. Shit, I hate these conflicting feelings inside of me right now. My brain feels like it's going to explode with confusion. I feel like I have something in common with this guy, because I also have lost my family, but at the same time, and for that same exact reason, I hate him. He disgusts me, and yet he makes me feel better about what has happened to me in the past. He makes me angry, and yet I feel like he is the key to digging up the skeletons which I have buried deep in an effort to avoid facing. My demons haunt me every day while I'm awake so just imagine what my nightmares are like.

What the hell am I supposed to do hey? I'm a friggen hoodlum for God's sake. I hate people like Matthew. I hate them, and I don't know why.

It's not all of them I hate—just the ones who killed my family. But my hatred has spilled out uncontrollably and my gang-life has corrupted any moral fibre that once existed in me. Deep down I feel dreadful about the bad things I've done and continue to do, but my conscience has long been ignored. It is only now that I can feel it clawing its way back into my consciousness, and I cannot stand it. I don't want it there.

It's terrifying.

I don't want to feel bad about taking the law into my own hands and creating my own justice system based on the injustices that were brought upon me. I can't feel bad about that because all pay-back I've given was fair. And just. I hate being here because it's playing with my mind and I despise that. I loathe it. I hate everything about this place and everyone here, but most of all, I hate myself.

Tomorrow, when the bus comes, I am gone.

Felicity: Oh, poor Matthew! I give him a massive hug just before we begin walking back to the shack. I can't believe the crap he's been through. His story has certainly made me think about how lucky I am. I know I take a lot for granted, but it's not my fault that I was born so fortunate, and pretty, and intelligent. Obviously I wasn't born lucky enough though because look at me now—I'm a mess!

Money isn't everything, I know that, but it certainly does help in life. I've never had to worry about money or anything like that, but I realise that not everyone has it so easy. Why can't the world just be more equal in its wealth? We could get rid of poverty. I've never even given to charity, so who am I to start questioning like that?! It would solve a lot of problems though. I read somewhere that we'd need an extra 7 or 8 earths to provide enough resources if everyone lived like I do. That's mind-boggling, but a bit far-fetched I think. But what would I know? I think I'm glad that I met Matthew—I usually screw my nose up at homeless people in the street and blame it on them for being so poor. For some people that may be true, but for others, like Matthew, I guess it isn't their choice.

Matthew's story certainly has had a drastic effect on me. I cried throughout it and had a weird, indescribable feeling in my tummy and chest. It also brought my defences down and I really need to talk to someone but I can't. I need to talk to someone because I am falling again. I feel like I am falling faster than ever before, and all because I feel bad about being so lucky. I am also very scared because I have nothing here to stop all these conflicting thoughts and feelings. I need my secret stash of pills from my bedroom at home. They always pick me up. I need my razor blade. The physical pain from cutting myself always numbs my mind and brings me back to a state of normality—if I can call that normal.

No! I don't need any of those things! They're just quick-fixes. I suddenly feel the pain in my thighs and I realise I'm clutching my wounds tightly so I let go.

I felt something new today when I was listening to Matthew's story and I cannot throw that away. I'm smarter than that. I know that I do not need anything to relieve my pain, but why can't I clear my mind of these alluring things that I wish I didn't yearn for? I cannot stop thinking about them! So many times have drugs and alcohol saved me from falling into a pit of darkness and self-destruction. Surely they're the reason I'm still here. They saved me from my depression, and helped me through the difficult times, right? They picked me up when I needed them most, when no-one and nothing else would. If all of this is true, then why the conflicting thoughts and feelings about how bad and evil those things are? I have these feelings inside of me that I do not understand—that if I return to my old ways, it'll be the last time I ever do, because I'll go too far.

Matthew: Wow, that was a much better reaction than I could ever have expected! Everyone seemed very interested in my story, and the girls certainly showed that they cared. Now as we walk back to the resort everyone seems to be deep in thought. Blake walks over to me and puts his arm on my shoulder.

"Thanks again Matthew," he begins, his grip tight around my shoulder. "We really appreciated what you shared with us and I think you struck a chord in everyone, including me. I would like to see the rest of your story on the video, if and when you feel up to it. And don't forget that I'm available 24/7 to chat okay?"

I smile and nod, and realise how important it was to everyone that I showed the video. I really hope the others show theirs soon. I'm very interested to see what their stories are. I hope they are not too ashamed or embarrassed to show theirs. I certainly was nervous, and also a little bit embarrassed, especially because most people avoid me as soon as they find out that I'm homeless, or a refugee. I guess these guys understand me, or feel my pain.

We sit in the dining room, having our tea in silence for the first time. No-one is arguing or bragging about anything, but also, no-one is even looking up from their plates. Blake watches us thoughtfully, and says a few things occasionally that none of us respond to, which doesn't seem to bother him. We're all a bit drained I think—physically and emotionally. It's actually nice to eat in silence. That way I can concentrate on enjoying this satisfying, delicious food! Plus it is much easier to straighten out my thoughts. I think about the events of the past few days, and about the others in my group, and then about Blake's book, which I finished reading last night. I reckon he chose that book for us to read for a reason—because it suits us all. The characters in the story have all been through many traumatic events but came out on top in the end by one means or another. I really hope that this is the same for us. I mean, it's easy to say that if we try our best, and live honestly, good things will come our way. But has Blake ever tried living on the streets for eight years? Has he ever been involved in a war, or had his neighbourhood terrorised? I doubt it. Once this rehabilitation program is over I'll have to go back to living on the streets with nothing gained but a few pieces of useless advice. I'm glad that I'm here because I can have some decent meals, but this free ride is not going to last forever. Yes, it is generous of Blake to be doing this, but he's basically fattening me up to feed me to the lions. I don't know how I'll survive once I get back.

By exposing myself today I also refreshed the deep hurt and rage inside myself—I miss my family so badly that I'd do anything, and I mean anything, to see them again.

CHAPTER 9

~ Running and Hiding ~

Felicity: I'm going to do it. I've decided that the time is right, and I must do it properly. It's now or never. I'm going to film my story before I can't take it anymore. I grab the camera and run through the paddock behind the clinic until I reach the scrubland. I want to make sure that no-one can see or hear me, just in case I don't even like what I might say. I have no idea what is going to come out, but if it worked for Matthew, then hopefully it'll work for me.

I set the camera up and sit there for at least half an hour trying to gather my thoughts. I have no idea where to start or if I even want to go through with this. I suppose it's because I have to do it. Or maybe it's because I want to. I don't know, but here goes.

I press the record button and face the camera, sitting myself down on a rock. I begin by telling them my name, Felicity Ellison, and where I live, Springfield, and that I am seventeen. I explain that I have no idea what I am about to say and if it will even be worth watching, but here goes nothing…

"I have taken drugs on and off for two years now. I have tried everything you can think of besides anything that needs to be injected. I take drugs because I feel bad about myself and my life, and to fill an emptiness I feel inside of me that I cannot explain. I also take them to numb the pain, and to make myself feel good. It helps me to forget certain things in my life, which I do not want to remember."

I pause for several seconds, staring off into the distance while considering what I am about to say.

"The major thing that caused me to choose this dangerous but tempting and addictive world of drugs was my younger brother Benjamin's death."

I wipe away a tear. Oh God, I'm already crying, I don't think I can handle this.

I take a deep breath, and then another, and try again.

"He was diagnosed with terminal cancer when he was nine, so we knew he wouldn't live to see the end of his teen years. The doctors and my parents explained this to me but I refused to believe them. My brother, tough little Ben—who was constantly annoying and bullying me even though he was half my size—was too young to die. It all happened way too fast. The diagnosis came, and then before I knew it he was dead. I just couldn't understand it and refused to believe he could die, even after he did. He died when I was fourteen, and it was then that my rational mind began to decay. I was diagnosed with depression at fifteen and that's when I used drugs to pick myself up for the first time. My parents sent me to get therapy, which didn't help at all because I lied about everything that I was asked."

I peel back my sleeves to reveal the many scars to the camera.

"Around the same time, I also began cutting myself. I don't know why I do it, but especially under the influence of mind-altering, but amazing substances, it just feels good. Cutting myself removes any pain and anguish that is tormenting me inside and I can feel it bleeding out of my wrists and evaporating. Quite a few times I would cut myself so badly that I would pass out. It became pretty much an everyday routine for me. My parents didn't even notice. Or if they did, they didn't say anything about it so I guess they didn't care.

My quick descent into this dark world also blinded me from the fact that my family was falling apart. After their beloved son died, and their daughter was becoming reckless, my parents changed for the worse. They stopped talking to each other and me, and seemed to live their own separate lives. I caught my dad sleeping with another woman one day when I came home early from school because I was sick. He told me not to tell mum or he'd kick me out onto the streets. I didn't really care if I ended up on the streets because I just wanted to get away, but I knew that I wouldn't be able to survive there. I'm not strong enough. I never did tell my mum, but I had a feeling she knew, because she always ignored dad and started arguments over nothing, and became a lazy slob, with the excuse of working from home. That's when dad didn't come home as much, and started going on more business trips. I was too caught up in my own problems, in my own pathetic world to even care or do anything about it."

I shake my head and realise that it's my fault that I've ended up like this. I took the easy way out by avoiding and ignoring the problems that faced me. But I still crave the feel of the cool blade against my skin. It sets me free.

"About a couple of months ago it was the third year anniversary of my brother's death. I usually go to his grave with flowers and prepare something to say, but this time I completely forgot. Instead, I went home and felt something different but frightening inside of me. That was the day I tried to kill myself."

I point to the scar on my throat.

"That's how I got this, and that's why I'm here. Now, what you've got to understand is that because of my choice to take drugs, many other bad things happened to me, which I will not go into much detail right now—I've already stirred up enough pain.

While under the influence I lost my virginity, was sexually assaulted, physically abused, and experienced some fairly severe ill health. All of the dreadful things I've mentioned today have been cluttering up my mind and making my depression worse, until that fateful day when I almost died. I still don't understand why I didn't die, but I'm glad I didn't. Because now I can finally face my demons."

I turn the camera off and wipe my face dry. I sit there for hours, letting everything that I just said sink in properly. I may never have said these things if I were still back home and I don't know what it is about this place that compelled me to do it. Maybe it's the peaceful setting we're in or the fact that there's a group of us all screwed in the head in some way. I dunno what it was, but something clicked inside me and out it spilled, my bitchy barrier unable to stop it this time.

Finally I decide it is time to go back to the clinic. I don't think I'm ready to show anyone the video yet, I don't know if I ever will, but at least it's done. It feels like I don't have such a burden on my shoulders now. And at least I was finally honest about my feelings.

Rebecca: This is cool! We're playing volleyball in the swimming pool and it's so much fun! I've never really played any sports so I'm not very good, but it is actually kinda fun. Blake is on my team and we're against Jason and Matt. Felicity just returned from her long walk and is watching us from the side, her legs draped into the water. She has a blank look on her face.

Jason spikes the ball and it hits Felicity, causing her to tumble into the water! Everyone laughs but she yells at him and storms off. It looked pretty funny, but I hope she's okay.

"We better get out soon," Blake announces. "The bus will be here in about half an hour."

Great, the bus is coming—with our visitors on it. But I don't have anyone to visit me, and I doubt Matthew does either. So I guess it'll be prissy little Felicity, and macho-man Jason who get to spend some time with their loved ones. The boys don't look too excited about this news either, although Jason's eyes light up a little. Maybe he's expecting someone. I figure there's no point running off and hiding, because the others will find out sooner or later that I've got no-one. Suddenly there is a sick feeling developing in my stomach that reminds me that there is one person who could possibly turn up—I'd rather die than see that sleazy asshole again. I shake my head and follow the others out to the front gate and wait for the bus. Felicity has changed her clothes and comes running to catch up with us. The boys are kicking around a football—they seem to be getting along much better lately.

Soon after, the mini-bus arrives and everyone is anxious to see who is on it. We stand near the door, unable to see inside because of the dark, tinted windows. The bus driver opens the door and hops down, turning to face us with a happy grin. He becomes more serious when he reveals the bad news—no-one has a visitor. Not a single person came to visit us! I suppose it is a good thing, we don't want to be tempted to run away. Where the hell would I go anyway? Nobody wants me. Nobody has ever wanted me. I don't feel upset at all, if anything I'm a little relieved that no-one showed up.

I look over at Matthew, and he looks very upset with his head down. I don't understand why he's upset, but I guess it reminds him of how much he misses his family. Yeah nice one Blake. You really thought this one through.

Jason doesn't look phased at all. He just walks off somewhere and disappears.

Felicity looks the most upset, almost like she is fighting back tears. I guess her family is too busy with their mansions and fast cars and parties or something. Maybe she doesn't even have a family, I don't know. She said she does, she was bragging about them at tea last week—maybe it was all lies. At least now she knows how we feel every day. The bus driver passes Felicity an envelope after calling out her name and she opens it quickly and reads the letter. As soon as she finishes reading it she throws the letter onto the ground and runs off, tears streaming down her face. I walk over and pick up the letter. It reads,

> "Dear Felicity,
> I'm sorry we couldn't make it to see you this week. Maybe we will next month. Grandpa is in hospital again and I need to stay here to look after Grandma. It's much too far to come just to see you for one evening! I'll try to at least write to you every week. I hope you're doing okay.
> I love you, I do. And so does your father.
> Love Mum
> Xoxo"

Oh my God. Felicity is so lucky. I wish my mum would actually write to me. I wish my mum would say that she loves me. I wish I knew my mum.

My heart starts to pound, and I mimic Felicity's move by dropping the note and running off. Blake calls out to me but I just keep going. I run for what seems like miles. I don't stop until I reach the caves at the other end of the beach, just on the other side of the massive sand dunes. I crawl into one of the caves and hold myself tight, panting to catch my breath and wishing that someone would come and take me far, far away from here.

Matthew: Well that bus visit was certainly very disappointing for everyone. I wonder why Blake didn't check if we had visitors or not. Surely he knows that most of us barely have anyone able to visit us anyway so there isn't any point having a visitors' bus. Not very well organised. Felicity and Rebecca looked really upset, I hope they're okay. I decide to go look for them and start in the most obvious place, their rooms. They aren't there, and I can't see Jason either. They can't be far off, so I guess I'll check the beach first. As I walk along the beach I hear the bus taking off again.

I walk as far as the biggest sand dunes and turn around to go back, but as I do I hear a tiny voice calling out to me. I turn around and see a small head poking out from one of the caves—Rebecca! She certainly found a good place to hide! I run over to her and see that she's been crying so I offer her my handkerchief—my only one, and I've never used it because it's my mother's. She wipes her eyes and nose with it and I tell her that she can keep it because she might need it later. I give her a hug and then she beckons for me to sit down. She looks like she's bursting to say something.

"I know what it's like Matthew," she says between sobs. "I've never met my family. I was put up for adoption at birth, and every foster family that took me in treated me like dirt. Not once have I felt loved in my life. After reading Felicity's letter, I realised how much I need that kind of attention. I crave it. But not just from anyone. I need it from my real family. I just wish I knew who they were."

Rebecca throws her arms around me and begins to cry her eyes out, so I tighten my arms around her. I had no idea she didn't have a family either. At least I know who my family is, but Rebecca hasn't even met hers. I don't know if I'd be able to handle that, so she must be really brave. I wonder what her foster families did to her. I hope they weren't too mean to her...

After at least an hour, she tells me she wants some alone time so I leave her and head back down the beach. Blake meets me when I arrive back at the resort.

"Where is everyone?" He asks, looking very concerned. I think he's realising that he's giving us too much freedom.

"I just spoke with Rebecca, she's down the beach. I don't know where Felicity and Jason are."

"I hope they get back in time for tea." Blake begins to smile. "We're having pizza and cake."

"Awesome! I can't wait!" I smile back at him and walk off to the common room where I find Felicity. She is watching a movie so I sit next to her.

"Wassup?" I try to be smooth and put my arm around her. I have no intention of kissing her or anything like that, but I just want to know if she's okay.

"Not much." She raises her eyebrows, wondering what I'm up to. "You?"

"Yeah, bout the same. You doin' okay?"

"Yep, thanks." She focuses on the television.

Well I don't need to be told twice that she doesn't want to talk so I sit there and watch the girlie movie with her, and I'll admit that I actually enjoy it! Halfway through the film, Felicity falls asleep on my shoulder. I smile—this is nice. I'm glad I've made a good friend. I wonder if we'll be able to keep in contact when we leave here. I mean, I don't have a phone or permanent address so it might be impossible. I'm sure we'll figure out something...

My daydreaming is interrupted by Blake bursting into the room.

"Sorry to interrupt," he begins, looking a bit frantic. "Jason is gone."

CHAPTER 10

~ *On The Run* ~

Jason: That was easy, too easy. I can't believe they left the bus unattended for me to waltz right onto it! I'm crouched down behind the seats at the back of the bus so unless the driver picks someone up and they see me I'm home free! I just hope it stops somewhere close to where I live. If not, I'll just have to steal a car or something. I wonder what the lads have been up to since I've been gone. Not having too much trouble from the Mayhem Crew I hope. I'll get them back though for shooting me. Nobody shoots *me* and gets away with it.

They will pay for it, believe me.

I'm just glad I'm not stuck in that depressing bloody hole anymore with nothing to do but listen to all the whingeing and crying. Why can't girls just get their emotions out like guys and punch or yell? I hate to say it, but part of me actually misses them already. Just the girls though—I don't think I'll ever miss Matty-boy. It took all my energy and strength to not bash him again. It's nothing against him personally… Well actually it is. I do have a personal vendetta against black people, but only because of what they did to me, to my family. I don't know if my feelings about this will ever change either, and for some reason, for the first time since it happened, I feel kind of guilty for thinking like this. Deep down I am beginning to realise how bad my racist attitude is. I am an intelligent guy and before the tragedy happened I would've despised people with attitudes like mine. My best friend throughout primary school was an African and he is a great guy. I also understand that there are good and bad people in every culture, but this hasn't altered the fact that I have this huge prejudice towards a whole culture, or colour. I never really thought about these factors until now—I have always been too blinded with rage and vengeance. Somehow though, today I feel a bit sick about what I have become.

What the hell did Blake do to me? That piece of shit! I punch the chair in anger. He must've brainwashed me because I don't feel normal anymore. I feel weak, tired, confused and angry. I think I'm angry for a different reason, but I don't know what it is and I don't like it. I want to ignore this conscience, I have to. I hope the lads don't notice any changes—it could be deadly for me if I say the wrong thing, even though I am the boss. It'll be fine. Once I get back into stealing, fighting, drinking, and gatecrashing parties I'll be back to normal.

A couple of hours later the bus comes to a stop so I sneak a peek out the window. I see a sign saying "Hillsburg Bus Depot". I sigh with relief—I am only one or two suburbs away from where I live. I wait until the bus driver is gone before I break out. I push out the rear emergency window, which smashes on the ground and sets off an alarm. I jump out and walk off casually, untroubled by the blaring alarm.

Felicity: Matthew and I jump up.

"What do you mean he's gone?" We both say in unison.

"He must've snuck onto the bus while we were unloading the supplies," Blake says, his face creased and pale with stress. He holds up a video tape. "He left this. There was a note with it saying—'I can't stay here. Show everyone the tape. Bye, Jason. P.S. Sorry for breaking your camera.' There's nothing more we could've done to stop him."

I stand there completely shocked. I knew Jason hated being here but I didn't think he would actually run away! What a wimp! I can't believe he chickened out and left just when we were beginning to get somewhere. I'm going to slap him if I ever see him again!

"I can't believe he's gone," Matthew says, looking just as stunned as me. "What are you going to do?"

"Nothing," Blake answers. "This is a voluntary program, so he didn't really have to sneak out like he did, although he probably did so to avoid being questioned by the police. We have to inform the authorities by law but that's all. We'll just watch his video and decide where to go from there. Can someone go find Rebecca please?"

Matthew nods and leaves immediately. I have nothing else to say. I am too shocked, but at the same time I know that if anyone was to run away it would be him. I kind of wish I had thought of running away too! I could've got away from all this but now I'm stuck here in this confronting program with not even the guts to show them my video.

At least if I did run away like Jason, I could leave the video here for them to watch as well, and not have to see their reactions, especially Matthew's. I'm afraid of him finding out that I take drugs, and hurt myself, among other horrible things. I don't think he's ever touched anything like that in his life, and he'll probably hate me if he found out. Although he's obviously aware there are some bad things about me that he doesn't know, otherwise I wouldn't be here in the first place. I don't know why I'm so worried about it because I barely know him. I guess I'm really becoming fond of him. He's just such a nice, genuine guy. At least he seems like it, from what I've seen. I guess he might have some deep dark secrets too.

Jason: As soon as I round my street corner and spot my apartment block I begin to sprint, excitement building up at the thought of finally being back home. I run up the stairs and bang on the door, hoping that my room-mate Jimmy is there. I can hear him swearing, as he is probably asleep or something. It's not my fault the bus got back so late! He swings the door wide open, and stands there topless, flexing his rippling muscles and brandishing a baseball bat. His angry face turns into a grin once he realises it's me.

"Jason!" He lunges forward and gives me a bear hug, showing his strength by lifting me up. "I was wondering when you'd show up!"

"Yeah." I breathe a sigh of relief for being home. "What's been going on?"

"Well champ, a whole bloody lot." We sit back down. He tosses me a cigarette after lighting his own. "The lads have been trying to find out where you were so that we could break you out. But no one's even heard of this rehab place! And what the hell do you need to go to rehab for anyway?"

"I'm addicted to beer and sex," I answer and we both laugh. "But nah man it wasn't that kind of rehab. They were trying to get to the bottom of our problems and all that bullshit."

Jimmy curses loudly and grinds his teeth in anger. I try to keep a neutral expression.

"That's rotten mate, completely rotten. I can't believe they made you go there! You're not the first person in the world to be shot!"

"Yeah I know." I take a drag on my cigarette and cough a little because it's been a while.

"We should go torch the place bruz." Jimmy spits.

"Waste of time. What happened to the Skinny?"

By Skinny, I refer to the thug who shot me. We call them *Skinnies* because of their natural build—tall and thin. Of course, not all of them are of this description, but enough for us to stereotype them in this way. One of the main Skinny gangs actually took this label and made it part of their gang name—*Skinny Gangstaz*. It just showed us that they don't care what we call them—they'll never be intimidated. They tend to call us *skinheads*, or *white trash*—also because of our appearance. Naturally they only call us the latter if they have the numbers, as they are not too brave on their own.

"Nothin'." Jimmy shrugs. "They disappeared because of the heat until just recently when they've been showing up looking for more trouble. They have teamed up with one of the Asian gangs from the north, and have been travelling around in force. They are after *you*,

Jason. They've enjoyed the freedom with you gone and they wanna make it permanent."

"I know," I say, knowing that my time was bound to come. I have been causing too much trouble for far too long and with the wrong people. "I guess it's rumble time then."

"Oh yeah baby!" Jimmy exclaims. A scantily-clad girl walks out of his room and asks if he is coming back to bed. He brushes her off. "In a minute, bloody hell. I'm talking to my mate here!" He winks at me and I nod in approval.

"We'll need backup though," I state plainly, feeling myself getting back into the rhythm already. "Especially if they already do. Send the word out—the rumble will be on Saturday night. Usual rules: no weapons, no trouble in the days beforehand, and the loser crew stays out of the others' territory *forever*. And no more trade between rival crews. This'll be the rumble to end them all."

Jimmy's eyes light up, and his usual dangerous look sweeps across his face.

"Oh man!" He bounces up in his seat like a child. "I can't wait to get those bastards back. I'll get all the lads together for it okay?"

"For sure." I nod, feeling the rush of adrenaline building already. I can understand why I became addicted to this life. "Get Jono's crew to back us up as well. He owes me a favour."

Jimmy nods and stares thoughtfully into space, while swinging his switchblade between his fingers. This makes me feel uneasy, and I have a sick feeling in my stomach. I don't like the look on his face. I know what he's like—unpredictable and reckless, much like the rest of the crew, but this time I fear the worst.

Rebecca: Matthew came to get me, which was sweet of him, and we are walking back along the beach. He told me that Jason has run away, which doesn't surprise me. I had a feeling he would. I don't think he wanted to be here at all, and he's the only one brave enough to do a thing like that. We walk into the meeting room, where Blake and Felicity are waiting. He asks me if I'm okay, and I just nod. He emphasises that Jason is not in trouble, but that we are watching his tape "as per his request".

The video begins with Jason holding the camera and jumping from rock to rock, pretending he's a stuntman or something. It's actually quite amusing! He then sets the camera down on a rock and sits opposite, with the cliff-face directly behind him. He looks very unsure about something, but finally begins:

"Hi everyone." He waves at the camera. "I can't believe you somehow convinced me to go through with this Blake!" He laughs and shakes his head before returning to his usual serious facial expression.

"You guys know me as Jason, but my full name is Nathaniel Jason Parker. Everyone these days just calls me Jason. Anyway, let me start by telling you about my family. I would never tell *anyone* this story usually, so I'll probably end up just destroying this tape, but who knows, you might get lucky... My dad was a detective in the police force, and was head of an elite taskforce whose aim is to crack down on gangs of all types. My mother was a teacher, and my brothers and sister were all in school. I loved them all to bits and still do. I always knew that I'd do anything for them, and protect them from anyone or anything. I'd give up my life for them... I just never thought that anything bad could ever happen to us, to my family."

Jason looks down, some dangerous anger evident in his wide eyes.

"Then one Saturday night I came home late from a party. As I walked up to the front door, four guys stormed out, knocking me to the ground. They were wearing balaclavas so I couldn't see who they were. But one of them stopped and pulled his off to reveal his face, grinning from ear to ear. He was a Negro, and not much older than I was. He looked at me and said—'time to join your family' in a blood-curdling evil voice and rammed a huge blade into my stomach."

Jason pulled his shirt up to show the scar, which was to the left of his bellybutton.

"I woke up a few days later in hospital with no recollection of how I got there. My best mate Dave was by my side, and he couldn't get it into my head that my family had been killed, no matter how many times I called out for them. I just refused to believe him."

Jason's voice begins to shake with fury. "Two of dad's cop friends came by and told me the story. Dad had been close to getting enough evidence to put the key players in a large Negro gang away for life—they had been involved in a string of murders or something major. Anyway, they had been threatening my dad for months, telling him to withdraw the case, but he refused—sometimes even at gunpoint. That's how brave my dad was. My younger siblings couldn't understand why we had to move house so often. To make things more complicated, the suspects hired members from a different Negro gang to kill my family. They walked right into my home while my family were sleeping and cut their throats. My parents both had evidence of torture, with puncture wounds and burns all over their bodies. My mum had signs of rape. They had stripped all of them naked, even my poor little beautiful baby sister."

Jason grinds his teeth together.

"She was only six."

Jason pauses for a moment to wipe his eyes dry. It is a heart wrenching sight—one of the toughest looking guys I've ever seen showing such real and raw emotion.

"They tortured them and killed them all without hesitation." He continues with obvious rage in his voice. "From the moment I heard how they died, from that very moment I made a pledge to hunt the bastards down...

And I did. I found them. I found those worthless pieces of shit. I took a few of my equally huge footy mates around to their houses and beat them all to a pulp. I didn't know exactly which ones did it so I had to torture the one guy I recognised. I didn't stop punching him until he gave me the name of the gang who had hired them. I left him with more scars than he gave me.

And so it began... I became obsessed with hunting down lowlifes like that. I was careful not to kill any of them though—I didn't want to lower myself to their level and give them the pleasure of being put out of their misery. I wanted them to feel the pain that my family felt moments before they were killed, and the pain that I felt when I realised I wasn't there to protect them—a pain which I live with *every* single day of my life."

He pauses and breathes in a huge lungful of air.

"So that's how it all began—my gang life, and I haven't stopped since. I don't think I'll ever turn back. I won't because I can't, and I can't because I won't. Don't ask me how that works, but I don't know any other way to explain it... It hurts though, deeper than any of you could ever imagine. I wish I was given away at birth so I didn't have to go through this pain and torment and carry this burden. I wish I could rewind back to that night and be there for them. For my family. To protect them... To die with them..."

His face is twisted with fury and he jumps up and kicks the camera, the footage shows some sky briefly before it comes crashing down to the ground and flashes to black.

Blake passes me a tissue and I realise that I, along with everybody else in the room, have been crying this whole time. Man, I've turned into such a cry baby!

"Well everyone." Blake blinks to try and dry his eyes. "I think that's enough for today. We'll discuss this another day okay? I think we all need some time to let this sink in."

We all nod and walk out of the room slowly, Matt with his arms around both us girls. I really want to give Jason a hug. I want to tell him my story now and talk with him about his. But now he's gone, and I can't. I don't know what to do. I haven't even started my video yet, and already two people have shown theirs. Blake said we don't even have to show anyone the footage so maybe I'll just leave it and see if I can get away with not doing it. I've already survived several weeks of this program so I'll just keep it up. I'll just keep on being the quiet one—even though talking to Matthew, and helping Felicity the other day when we were bushwalking, both made me feel good inside. But I know that it is pointless to feel good, even just for a moment, because as soon as I finish here I'll be back working at that evil, dirty, jail-like brothel. I'm surprised Mr. Trig hasn't come and found me, seeing as I earn him the most money. Well, not so much these days, because I'm getting older, but when I first started there, which I can barely even remember, I certainly got the most customers...

Oh, God...

I suddenly feel light-headed and sick so I run into the girls toilets and throw-up in the sink.

These are the terrible thoughts and memories that haunt me every day.

CHAPTER 11

~ *One Step Forward, Two Steps Back* ~

Matthew: I lie here on the sand looking up at the stars, thinking about the past couple of days. I still can't believe that Jason ran away, but after watching his video I think I'm beginning to understand why. It must've been hard for him being here with me. To him, I must look just like the guys who killed his family. I guess that's why he beat me up. That and the fact that he is a thug. I wonder if being here helped him at all, but I doubt it. He wanted to get out from the first day—I could see it in his eyes. He also wanted to kill me as soon as he saw me! I wonder where he is now and if he got straight back into his old life without thinking of the consequences. I have no idea what gang life is all about but I've seen my fair share of it from living on the streets and from what I've gathered, it all leads down the same bad road. I remember seeing one group of about nine or ten young hoodlums attack another group of only three. I think that is totally unfair and cowardly, and I hope that's not what Jason gets into. I've never been in a proper fight before, but most of the ones I've seen have been between two people who slog it out while the rest watch. Then once the fight is over, one of them buys the next round of drinks. That's the way it should be I think—fair and safe. That's the way real men should fight. I don't know how likely that is to happen though. Guys usually won't accept when they lose. I continue thinking about the many things I have seen on the streets, until my tiredness takes over and I fall asleep, still lying on the sand.

* * * *

Blake rolls over and hugs his wife from behind. Anne smiles contently.

"I just hope Jason is okay," Blake says to her, while stroking her long blonde hair. "I hope we got through to him somewhat at least."

"I know you did," she answers reassuringly. "It is evident on the video that he is thinking about his life, and the path he has chosen to take. You may never see him again, but rest easy knowing that you did your best."

"Thanks sweetie." Blake sighs and rolls over again to stare at the ceiling.

"Jacob would be proud," Anne says and snuggles up to him. Blake smiles at her and nods.

"I hope so."

Jason: It is only two days to the big rumble and all I can think about still is Blake, Rebecca, Felicity, and even Matthew. It's a strange feeling not being able to get these people out of my head. I just want to keep hating them—it's so much easier. I just wish I thanked them for their help. I finally told my story to someone and it actually feels good. Only my mate Dave knows the full story, and I've since lost contact with him. The other lads that I roll with now just know I'm a hard-nut and they're not interested in my sob story, no matter how dramatic it is.

Jimmy bursts into my room, full of energy as usual, and jumps onto my bed, nearly hitting his head on the ceiling fan.

"Hey champ! What's up?"

"Nothin' Jimmy," I reply, feeling awkward, like he could read my thoughts. "Kate came by earlier today, while you were asleep.

She said that Kelly is doing fine, and that she needs to talk to you about child-support."

"Oh great." I pretend to be uninterested, but I actually really want to see my daughter. "How'd she find out that I was back anyway?"

"Are you crazy man?" He looks at me amused. "You're the buzz of the town. Even the police came looking for you yesterday while you were out on the piss! They want you to get into contact with them or some rubbish."

"What for?" This news annoys me because the cops are always bothering me. Anytime something big goes down in this area they come to me for information, which I never give them even if I do know something. "Because I left rehab early or something?"

"Probably, I dunno." Jimmy shrugs and gives me a playful shove. "You've been a naughty boy!"

"What's new?" We both laugh, but I feel very down for some reason. I've never really thought much about anything in life—it's too painful. But recently I think about everything.

"Well dude." I jump up off the bed. "I'm gonna go to Kate's then and see my little Kelly."

"A'ight," Jimmy replies and gives me our gang's patented handshake. "Catch you later bro."

I decide to walk seeing as Kate only lives a couple of blocks from my apartment. We were together for about a year, and broke up just after she told her parents that she was pregnant, which was over a year ago. They pretty much forced her to break up with me and tried to convince her to have an abortion. Her dad can get violent sometimes and they were arguing about the whole situation right in front of me one day and he slapped her really hard, one of his rings cutting her face. I fired up and shoved him hard and he fell backwards onto a glass coffee table, smashing it as he landed. I haven't been back to their house since. I didn't see much of Kate until the birth, which I made sure I was at, against her parents' protests. She made sure I got to see Kelly as much as I could, but the last time I saw her was three months ago on my birthday. I don't know if Kate and I will ever get back together, but we'll try to share bringing up Kelly. Kate wants Kelly to know her father from an early age.

I spot Kate's house in the distance and start sprinting, excited about seeing Kelly, but also nervous because of her parents. I hope they're not home. I notice a "For Sale" sign on the front lawn, which makes me hesitate.

I knock on the door, and her dad promptly answers it. As soon as he sees me he tells me where to go and begins to slam the door.

"Wait," I say, putting my arm across the door to stop it from closing. "I need to see my baby. Please."

Mr. Marshall hesitates but reluctantly gives in.

"She's in her room." He gestures upstairs, so I jog up, taking three steps at a time, ignoring Mr. Marshall's rule of "no running in the house".

I knock on her door and after no answer I push the door open. Kate is sitting on her bed blow-drying her hair. She looks up and is startled at the sight of me, nearly dropping the dryer.

"Jason!" She runs over to embrace me. I hesitate but then hold her tightly. "I've missed you so much."

"I know." I semi-smile at her. "Where's Kelly?"

She hops over to the cot and picks my cute little baby up, passing her to me.

I look down and admire her innocence and beauty. I can't believe I helped create something so perfect, and yet look at the tragic world we've brought her into. I'm so afraid of Kelly growing up and seeing everything that I've seen. But what else can I do? It's all part of life I guess. If only it didn't have to be.

"Nath," Kate whispers. She is the only person I will allow to call me that since my parents died. "I need to talk to you." She beckons for me to sit next to her on the bed, so I follow, still cradling my precious little one.

"What's with the for sale sign?" I ask Kate but she isn't listening.

"I want to get back with you," she begins, her eyes lighting up with the prospect of starting anew. "But my parents say we can only do so if you quit your gang. For good."

"Kate." There's a firmness in my voice. "You know very well what will happen if I quit my gang. I told you what happened to the last traitor. There's no way that I can do it, even if I want to."

"We can run away from here, and start a life somewhere else!" Kate says desperately trying to persuade me.

"It's just not possible!" I hang my head, knowing that I can never escape this life. "I guess you heard about the rumble."

She nods, her excitement fades to fear.

"You don't have to go Jason." She grips my hand tightly. "Stay here with me. Please, don't do it!"

"It's my fault this rumble is on!" I push her hand away. "They have a beef with me, and there's nothing I can do about it but this."

Kate looks very disappointed in me, and grabs Kelly back who has started crying. I understand how much of a bad idea this rumble is, but I also know there's no way out of it.

"I'll come around once it's over," I try to reason with Kate. "We'll talk about everything then and I'll even tell you about this rehab place."

"Don't bother, Jason." She won't even look me in the eye now. "And you need to leave now. I'll contact you about child support soon."

She turns away from me until I leave her room, and she slams the door shut behind me.

I run all the way back home, but this time I take a detour past my old church—another place I haven't visited since that fateful night. I refused to believe that if God really existed he would let such a horrible thing happen. So I came to the conclusion he doesn't exist, which doesn't explain the many nights I've spent yelling into space in anger blaming him for everything.

I stand outside the huge double doors and look at the tall steeple. I've never really prayed before, even when my parents took me to church. I just pretended to, thinking it was a big joke and pointless but I guess I could give it a go now. I've got nothing to lose.

God, if you're there. If you are listening, I need your help. I don't know what to do. I don't know how you can help me, but my parents used to take me to church, and there's gotta be a reason they did. I know I've been angry at you because you took them from me. I've hated you for a long time for that. You took them from me and left me all alone. I've never understood why you allowed that to happen, and I don't think I ever will. But now I think I finally understand what I must do. Help me get through this rumble on Saturday night; help me survive it, so that I'm not taken away from my baby girl. I don't want her to know the pain of losing a loved one before she even gets to know me... Well that's it. Peace.

I don't even know if that was pointless or not, but at least it helped me get some things off my chest that have been bugging me for ages. I guess it's a little bit like when my sister used to write in her diary every day. She would write everything in there, not that a six-year-old would have much to worry about. If only she knew.

Felicity: I just showed my video to Blake in my session with him. I expected to get lectured about lying to him but he didn't even mention it. He just asked if I was okay and said he is glad I showed it to him. When I'm ready to show it to the group I will. But not before I add something extra, which I left out the first time. I didn't lie at all, but I may have omitted one big detail—probably the biggest detail. I don't know if I should even tell anyone. It's not really any of their business, even Blake's. And it is very personal—only our family and closest friends know about it and we promised to keep it that way, for our sake and Ben's. I really hope I can say it because I've never ever said it out loud. I don't know what the consequences would be if I did, but maybe this is the safest place to do so because I cannot run to my drug stash or my beloved razor blade.

I burst out into tears just thinking about what really happened to Ben, and I run down the beach, til I find my favourite spot in the sand dunes. I look out at the ocean and watch the waves crashing into the old ruined jetty pylons, amazingly still standing, but more beautiful than ever, after so many years of abuse. I decide it's warm enough for a swim, and the water looks amazing—crystal clear, sparkling over white sand, shining in the morning sun. As I dive in, a cold shock gets sent through my whole body. Man, I wasn't expecting it to be this cold! Oh well, it's refreshing. When I surface, I notice the others walking along the beach with Blake. I call out to them to come join me, so they strip down to the appropriate swimwear and run into the water—Rebecca walks in slowly and cautiously. Everyone immediately looks refreshed and we start splashing each other, and Matthew and Blake try to dunk each other.

"This place reminds me of home," Matthew says after coming up from being dunked by Blake.

"Cool, your country must be beautiful," I say to him. I notice him checking me out in my bikini, quickly looking away when I bust him.

"Yes," he replies a bit awkwardly. "I just wish I could go back there and help out. I hate being stuck here knowing that the poverty is spreading. I feel useless."

"You can you know," Blake says. "The fighting in your country stopped a few years ago. Allied forces went in there to try to restore peace and order."

"I know," Matthew says, a bit narky. "They didn't want a repeat of Rwanda I guess. It still took them a long time to respond though, once thousands and thousands had already been slaughtered." This is the first time I've seen Matthew get so defensive about something. Blake certainly struck a nerve! "But how am I supposed to get there? It's not like I can afford a plane ticket or anything!"

"Matt, I can help you out," I say, referring to my dad's disposable income.

"No." He looks at me in disgust before he turns and wades back to shore. "I don't want your charity! I've survived well enough so far, so just keep your damn dirty money!"

Whoa, where the hell did that come from? I think I struck a nerve as well there, and suddenly I feel sick in the stomach and want to just lie down and drown myself.

"Blake, I didn't mean to…" I try to defend myself.

"It's okay Felicity," Blake reassures me. "He's just very sensitive about the subject. He has more issues than he lets on about okay? Just like the rest of us."

That last comment hit me hard, especially with the curious look Blake gave me. Maybe he could sense that I wasn't telling the whole truth in my video. Or maybe he really was just referring to Matthew and I'm just being paranoid. It feels like I've got "liar" written on my forehead for everyone to see. And I thought Matthew was okay about being here. I didn't realise he was homesick—it never even occurred to me. I just assumed that all he wanted was his family, and I really wish I could help him find them. I really wonder why he hasn't found them yet. I wouldn't know where to start. I thought we were friends and that we could talk about anything. I guess I haven't been totally honest with him either. I wonder what else is bothering him though…

We walk back to the shack for some lunch and on the way I decide that it's time I show Matthew my video.

Rebecca: I hate it when people fight or argue. It makes me nervous and sick inside. There were always arguments at the brothel, either with the boss or a disgruntled customer. Quite often it would turn ugly, and it was us girls who received the brunt of it.

I hope Matthew is okay and that Felicity learns to mind her own business a bit. I mean, I know we are supposed to all be friends here and support each other, but she was pretty much just rubbing her wealth in his face and that he will never be as lucky. I hate that. I bet she thought she was being nice though, boasting about her money like that. It even makes me feel bad about how much money I have, which isn't much. Well it's actually nothing now, probably, unless I go back to work for Gus, or as he likes to be called, Mr. Trig. Just remembering that very name makes me shudder. It makes me even sicker inside, and it also makes me feel very angry. The anger is soon overwhelmed with frustration because I feel useless as I know I'll never be able to do anything to stop what that slimy, evil man does. God, why does everything have to remind me of him! I hate it.

I walk past Felicity and Matthew in the hallway. They certainly made up quickly! She better not be rubbing it in his face again. She must be very manipulative, or else he is just too nice. He probably just can't resist her charm.

"Rebecca!"

Man, what does she want now? I turn around impatiently and Felicity beckons for me to join them.

"I'm going to show Matthew my video," she tells me. Man she is so fake. I can see right through her scheming ways. "Do you want to come and watch it with us? I'd like that."

"Okay, whatever." I shrug. I could do with some entertainment. Let's see what the rich bitch has to offer.

She leads us to the common room where she sets it up to play on the big screen television. I roll my eyes—I guess she's not used to smaller TVs where she comes from. She presses play and sits close to Matthew, trying to snuggle up to him—he doesn't seem to mind. I shake my head and focus back on the TV and watch her short, but to the point video. I wonder how much of it is true or if she's just seeking attention.

"Aw, thanks for that Felicity," Matthew says and gives her a big, lingering hug, while I stand there awkwardly. "I really appreciate you showing that to us. At least I can finally begin to understand you!" He laughs, and she smiles. I wonder what he thinks about the drug abuse and self-harm part. I wonder if he still likes her. She looks over at me now, waiting for my comment.

"Yeah, thanks for that," I say, sounding just as fake as I think she is. "I'm here if you need to talk okay?"

Oh God, I can't believe I just said that! I wonder if even she heard though—I spoke pretty quietly.

"Thanks Rebecca." Felicity smiles at me. "That means a lot."

Yep, she heard alright. I just hope she doesn't come to me now for advice or anything. I wouldn't know what to say. I wish I hadn't said that now. She's still a spoiled stupid rich bitch. Wow, so she lost her brother and she's still not over it. I don't even know if I have a real brother.

Suddenly I feel the pain and fear building inside me again. I don't know why I hate being around people so much, but it's not getting any better, no matter how hard I try. In fact, I think it might be getting worse.

CHAPTER 12

~ Decision Time ~

Jason: This past week has been a massive blur. It feels like ages since I ran away from the clinic, but it was only on Tuesday. Now, I lie here in my bed, as I have done all day, fretting about going to the rumble tomorrow night. I cannot believe all of this is happening. I know it's my fault I'm in this mess, and sometimes I'm glad and happy to be in this life, but right now I have so many conflicting thoughts that I wouldn't know where to begin explaining them. I jump out of bed and throw on a wife-beater.

"Hey there sleepyhead!" Jimmy says as I walk out the front door without replying. I wish he was right about that description because I actually haven't slept properly in days.

I walk down to the local deli and buy a packet of cigarettes. I feel bad as I light one, but promise myself that I'll give up as soon as I get back with Kate. I walk down to the basketball courts to see if any of the boys are playing and I find Joseph, Tooth, Mike, and Benny there.

"Hey hey, look who it is!" Tooth comes running over to greet me. We call him "Tooth" because he is always getting into fights and barely has any of his original teeth left. He is one of the most fearless, hardest blokes I've ever met.

"Hey big fellah," I say to him. I turn to greet the others. "Hey guys, what's up?"

"Nothin' much," Benny shakes my hand, nearly crushing it from his mammoth size and strength.

"Good to see ya sir!" Joseph imitates a salute, laughs, and then shakes my hand.

"G'day champ." Mike puts his huge, tattooed arm around my shoulder. "Nice to have ya back."

"Ready for the big rumble?" Tooth asks me and pretends to box with Mike.

"I was born ready," I answer, trying to sound confident.

"Yeah, too easy," Joseph says, picking up the basketball and passing it to me. "We're gonna slay us some Skinnies!"

I shoot the basketball, trying to ignore Joseph's last comment. We play three-on-two for a while, with Joseph and me on one team as we are the best players. After several slam dunks and thrashing the other three, I decide to walk home. The boys offer to come but I refuse—I need some more time to think. I haven't had a clear thought in a long time and recent events haven't helped. I walk around every single day wondering what life would be like if my family was still here.

As I stroll down a side-street alone I wonder if it was the right decision to refuse the lads offer to escort me, as I notice a black four-wheel-drive following me at walking pace. I hope the 4wd's occupants know the rules of a rumble, particularly no causing trouble beforehand. There will be absolute mayhem if any rules are broken.

I keep walking as I light another cigarette and hope they stop following so that I can begin to head the right way home. I think they're expecting me to run—they obviously don't know me. After a couple of blocks of stalking, the 4wd screeches to a stop beside me, and five Skinnies jump out and charge at me. I take a long drag on my cigarette before dropping it and stand completely still, hoping that this is over with quickly. The first one lunges at me, tackles me to the ground and sits on my chest. He has a fairly slim build, and would never usually be able to knock me down, but I figure that it is safer to just let him win this time. The others form a circle around me, throwing taunts and curses at me.

"Why hello Jason," one of the Skinnies says and steps forward. I immediately recognise him. He is the one who shot me. I would never forget that face, with the long scar from his eye to his chin. "What are you doing walking around these parts alone? Not a very smart thing to do for a man whose head is wanted."

The other Skinnies sneer, and the one who shot me pulls out his infamous gun.

"You remember this don't you," he states coldly. "Yes, you are old friends. Why don't you say hello?" He pushes the gun into my cheek, then down my neck, and then to the spot where he shot me. He appears confident behind the protection of his weapon, unlike last time when he was quivering so much I am surprised he was able to pull the trigger.

"We don't have time for some stupid rumble so let me just end it right here, right now. You knew this was coming Jason. I dunno why you and your weak, piss-ant, mangy crew think you can continue to mess with us. You have no idea who we've joined forces with. We are more powerful than you can even imagine and we will annihilate you tomorrow night. So let me save the blood of the rest of your pathetic gang by just finishing you off now…"

I give the Skinny my hardest stare and push the other one off me.

"Well then," I say to him. "What are you waiting for? Just do it, you scumbag." I realise that there is nothing I can do, so I accept the consequences of my past actions and will take what I deserve. Usually I would put up a fight. I always said I would if I were ever in this situation—better to die fighting than running away like a wuss. But this time I won't run, and I don't want to fight. I just wish I could've held Kate and Kelly in my arms one last time and told them I loved them…

"Say hi to your family for us…" The Skinny cocks the gun and places it next to my temple. I close my eyes, and for the first time in years my mind is completely free.

A single gunshot echoes throughout the neighbourhood.

Jason: Suddenly, I no longer feel the gun next to my temple. I open my eyes and see smoke coming from Joseph's gun. He shot the Skinny in the hand—I'm glad it was him who was the shooter, and not reckless Tooth! The Skinny screams as they all bolt back to their 4wd and screech off while being bombarded with rocks thrown by the other lads. Joseph fires off a few more rounds into the back window.

"Bloody hell Jason! Are you okay?" Mike runs over to me.

"Of course champ," I brush myself off and turn to Joseph. "Thanks man."

He just nods and checks his gun. Benny comes running over after chasing the 4wd down the street.

"I don't think he'll be fighting tomorrow night!" I say and the other boys laugh. That was a close call. I'm glad for friends like these guys, even if they are extremely rough and violent. These guys are smarter than they look and they certainly value loyalty, respect for one another and friendship—traits that most people wouldn't pick just by looking at them. This is the life they've chosen to live, as have I, and I would never give up their friendship. However, I have come to realise many things this past week, and there's one thing that's perfectly clear to me right now—I'm not ready to die yet.

I've barely even started living.

Matthew: Gee, I had no idea what Felicity has been through. I know how she feels—I watched my sister die as well. I also lost a brother, but who's keeping count? But I never turned to drugs, no matter what I went through. And she cuts herself? What's with that?! I don't think I'll ever understand what that's all about. I'm not sure whether she even understands why she does it. She is extremely pretty, but now I can see her corrupted interior. Gosh, that must've been hard for her to show that, especially after hearing about the horrible things that Jason and I have been through. Oh there I go again, comparing whose life is worse or better. It's ridiculous and stupid for me to be thinking like this. We are all supposed to be equals in life, no matter what our stories are. I guess I've never felt equal before, or even better off than someone. I realise that I only want to have the worse story because I want to have the better, more heartbreaking one. I've never had recognition for anything and maybe that's a way to gain some attention. I don't know how that works but it's just how I feel. I've got to stop thinking about things so much! I wonder why Rebecca hasn't shown her movie.

I look at the clock in my room and realise it's time for the guest speaker, which Blake has organised, so I head down to the hall. Everyone is already there so I take a seat beside Rebecca. Felicity leans forward and smiles at me. I smile back even though I have mixed feelings about her now.

Felicity: Oh thank God Matthew doesn't hate me now. I thought he would certainly hate me after he found out my deep, dark secrets. I lean back in my chair and wait for the guest speaker to start talking. His name is Keith something—I didn't catch his last name. He begins talking about his past experiences, about how he was addicted to drugs and ended up in jail for armed robbery. He only stole to support his habit and thought that there was no other way out. In jail many bad things happened to him. He describes his horrific first night, where he was put into a cell with six other men who were violent, horny and soul-less. Enough said. He says that after a few months of being "broken in", the other inmates eased up on him and accepted him into their group. The first thing he noticed was that the prisoners were divided into their own ethnic and social minorities. No one talked to anyone from different groups unless it was to taunt them or to do a deal. There were fights every single day, usually over nothing but racial differences. He said he hated seeing all this crap going on but the best thing about it was that he got over his drug addiction. He had to give up cold turkey, which made the first month or two even more horrible, but after that he says he'd never felt better. He says he would rather experience the symptoms of drug withdrawal, even though the effects are worse than taking the drug, than stay a slave to it. He also began to read and enjoy the simple pleasures in life, which he had been blinded from by drugs and lust. He avoided all conflict in the prison, even when it was directly targeted at him. He was eventually labelled a "pussy", and his group disowned him, so he was stuck there all alone. But it wasn't long until he found some more prisoners who felt the same way as him. They too were in jail for bad choices that they regretted and together they all decided to make better choices from then on instead of giving up like everyone else had. It would be hard, but they'd be better off in the end. They became close friends, despite their cultural differences, and even wrote a book together, which became a bestseller.

His story took a turn for the worse, as it seems they always do, when he said that his mate Lawrence, a black man, was brutally murdered by another inmate, for no reason at all. Keith says he could see the darkness in the offender's eyes—the lack of remorse.

It stung him deeper than anything he could ever have imagined. All he could think about was avenging the death of his friend, but no matter how much he wanted to, he just couldn't do it. He doesn't know why, but he forgave the murderer and the day he was released he felt like he was born again. He could live his life again, on his terms, not controlled by anyone or any substance or anything.

A round of applause—good on you Keith. But what the hell has that story got to do with me? Besides the drugs part of course. It's almost as if this speaker was targeted at Jason, but I'm not sure it would've been a good thing. Probably would've just fired him up so it's a good thing he's not here hey.

I wonder if Blake purposely brought him in here to remind us of how bad we are, how bad I am? That's totally unfair and I feel like crap now, thanks Blake. I know I've got to quit taking drugs but it's so hard! As soon as I get back, I know I'll go straight for my stash. But I haven't really felt the need very much since I've been here. Only a couple of times I've wished I had my precious pills with me. That's really weird. Maybe it was different for Keith though. Maybe he was addicted to heroin or something. I'm not that bad am I? Why does Blake want us to hear all these sad stories? I know Keith's has a happy ending but does he seriously think that we'll all have the ideal endings? He's got to be delusional. He can't possibly expect to change us completely in a few short months and then send us back into the wild world and transform the way we were living. I mean, it wouldn't be so hard for myself to be okay out there, and possibly Rebecca, although I have no idea what her story is, but Blake is being a bit unfair by putting all of these hopes and dreams into Matthew's mind. Matthew may never see his family again and may have to live on the streets for the rest of his life! Did Blake even consider that? I bet he didn't. He's probably fantasised about saving us all from the evil things in our lives and then he can feel good about himself and hold his head up high. He's got no idea what we've been through, and I don't know why he even bothers trying.

Rebecca: I glare at Felicity chatting away with Matt like everything is okay. I bet she doesn't even have depression, like she says in her video. It sure doesn't look like it!

"Rebecca." Blake touches my shoulder which startles me. "Would you like to meet Keith?"

I turn to shake Keith's outstretched hand.

"Nice to meet you Rebecca," he says politely.

"Hi," I say, suddenly feeling vulnerable and self-conscious.

Blake introduces Keith to the others and then we head outside for a barbeque tea. Keith chats away to everyone but I avoid him as I don't really want to talk. I kind of miss Jason. I feel more comfortable and confident when he's around, even though he's a bit scary. I guess I built some sort of bond with him when he saved my life.

I try to avoid eating but Blake passes me a plate full of food. I don't know why I'm punishing myself but I haven't eaten in two days, even though the food looks and smells delicious. I figure that with no access to any form of substance to help me forget my troubles, starving myself is a good enough substitution. Blake begins to talk to me so I figure I've got to eat this. Maybe I'll be able to throw it up later.

"Any thoughts on what you heard from Keith?"

I sigh, partially because I am sick of Blake asking what I think, and also because of something that Keith had said. He mentioned going cold turkey. I remember vividly what happened to me when I stopped taking my drugs so suddenly. My body was sent into a state of shock and my delirious mind fought against me every single second of every day. The only thing that actually kept me going was the knowledge that by the end of that painful week I would be able to escape from hell. Keith said he had become trapped in the drug-life due to an addiction. For me, it was also an addiction, but mainly a means to temporarily forget I existed.

"Yeh, I dunno," I finally answer Blake. "I guess I didn't realise how many people there are with struggles. It's a sad world."

Whoa, that was totally out of the blue. I'm beginning not to care what I say to Blake, or anyone else. I'm over caring.

"Yes that's true. But we can change it for the better, one person at a time. Now eat that food!"

I begin eating and before I know it, the plate is empty. Wow, I feel better already! Blake notices my empty plate, smiles triumphantly and then walks off. Has he noticed that I haven't been eating? I hope not. How embarrassing! Oh well, he can't follow me into the toilets and stop me from sticking my finger down my throat. I head to the female bathroom and lean over the toilet. As I am ready to put my two fingers down my throat someone else comes in. It's Felicity, and I can hear her humming to herself as she goes to the loo next to me. She must've seen me come in here because she starts talking to me.

"Bec, is that you?" She calls out to me. Nobody's ever called me Bec before.

"Yes," I respond, pretending to sit down on the toilet and do my "business".

"What did you think of the speaker?" She asks me. I feel a bit weird having a conversation while in the toilet! Is this what she does with her friends?

"Yeah he was interesting," I reply, trying to avoid encouraging her to continue the conversation. We finish in the toilet, wash our hands and walk out together.

"I'd like to get to know you more," Felicity says to me. I'm not sure if she is being genuine but at least she's trying to be nice. "You seem really cool, and I think that us girls have got to stick together."

I just look at her with an obviously stunned expression on my face.

"If that's okay with you of course," Felicity adds after noticing my reaction.

"Yeah, sure," I reply, hesitant about becoming closer friends with her. I thought I might like to, early on in the week, when we were bushwalking, but that was only for a brief moment. Now I don't know whether to trust her, or just go along with it and maybe make my first proper friend.

CHAPTER 13

~ Face The Truth ~

Felicity: "Cool, come on then," I beckon to Rebecca to hurry up as we head down to the beach. I run ahead and she follows but looks very bothered about something. I take her to my favourite spot on the top of a tall sand-dune where we sit and watch the sun as it disappears over the distant edge of the ocean.

"How amazing is this place?" I say to her. I honestly am beginning to really warm up to it. When I was younger I used to hate the gritty feeling of sand between my feet. Now I think I have grown to love it.

"Yep, it's pretty nice," Rebecca says, still sounding shy and uneasy around me for some reason. We sit there in awkward silence for a while until I decide to find out what is wrong.

"Look, Bec," I begin. "I know that I may seem like the luckiest girl in the world because my family is so well off and everything, but all of that doesn't make me happy. Most of my so called 'friends' back home are only friendly to me because they like to come over and use all of our expensive stuff and swim in our indoor swimming pool. But I didn't ask for any of this, and sometimes I even wish that we weren't so wealthy, because then I would know who my true friends are. I want to feel wanted for who I am, and what I have to offer besides my material items. That's why I like you so much Bec. You are the only girl I've met who hasn't asked me to let you come over to my house to hold a party there, to spot you a fifty, or to see how many boys we can hook up with. And I like that."

I look at Rebecca and smile. I feel better now after saying that. I never realised that's what I truly thought about my so-called friends back at home until I heard myself say it. I guess I just wanted to deny it. Rebecca looks stunned, but her eyes have widened and I think she might be crying a little bit but it's getting too dark to tell. I can barely make out her facial expressions. She puts her hand on my arm and smiles. Her touch sends a shiver down my spine, like it's the first real touch from a friend, and not a fake one with an ulterior motive.

"Bec, even though you are really shy and quiet, and I don't know much about you, please know that you can tell me anything okay? But don't feel pressured. It is so much easier to tell secrets to a camera rather than an actual person, I can tell you that right now!" Rebecca smiles again and nods. I don't know if she'll ever tell me her story, not the full one anyway, but I can respect that, and I won't pressure her about it anymore.

Rebecca: Wow, I am shocked, I truly am. I seriously think Felicity is being genuine, and that she actually does want to be my friend. That thought alone just makes me want to cry. I can see now that she is a nice person, which I've rarely seen in such a pretty girl. The prettiest girls I know are all bitches. I guess you should expect that with the line of work I'm caught up in. This is a surprising and pleasant change. I can't let my guard down though, or else I could easily be hurt again. I want to tell her things. I want to tell her everything. But I don't know where to begin, and whether she'll still want to be my friend once she hears it. I've told Matthew a few things but not much. What if he tells Felicity and then she gets angry at me for not telling her? It'll ruin the only real friendship that I have ever been close to having. Well it can't hurt to tell her something. Anything. But what…

"It's okay Bec." Felicity looks at me, her eyes wide. "You don't have to tell me anything. I can just sit here and talk about any old crap if you like? I won't drill you with a hundred questions! I just want to…"

"Felicity," I interrupt her. "I'm a prostitute."

I don't know whether to be offended or relieved by the astonished expression on Felicity's face. I guess it's nice to not look like a working girl and have people jump to conclusions about what I am before I even have a chance to explain things.

"It wasn't my choice though," I say to try and reassure her. "I don't really remember how it all started, but I was on the streets by the time I was twelve after running away from a foster home, and I nearly died out there. I don't know how Matt does it, being homeless, but I couldn't survive. And I was desperate. The only person who would take me in was the very person who ended up destroying what little sense of life I had left…"

I can't hold the tears in, and I start sobbing heavily. Felicity puts her arms around me, pulls me close and holds me tight so that I feel safe.

"It's okay sweetie." She tries to comfort me. "I understand. You're safe now okay? You're safe here."

These few, simple words of comfort penetrate deep inside me and begin to warm up my tender, delicate, heavy heart. I feel a new warmth developing inside of me, one that I've never felt before. My mind is beginning to straighten out, and my feelings of anger and hatred have been eased for the moment. I've been too scared to tell anyone the truth about myself, but now I think it'll be okay. Felicity didn't run for the hills after hearing the news, or put me down or judge me in any way. I feel like spilling my whole story to her and getting it all out in the open so that I can deal with the constant gnawing inside of me. My rotting interior feels like it is subsiding. But I know that this feeling won't last long either—I can already feel it dying down. I need to get my story out while it is fresh in my mind right now. I peel myself away from the comfort of Felicity's arms and jump up.

"I've gotta go. Thanks for the talk."

I begin to run. I run all the way back to the resort without slowing down. I didn't even hear Felicity call out to me, maybe she didn't. I run straight past Blake, who tries to ask me something, and on up to my room where I grab the camera. I need to find somewhere safe and secluded to film this with no distractions or interruptions.

It is time.

Matthew: "Gee, she was in a hurry!" I say to Blake as Rebecca runs off again, this time clutching her camera bag.

"Yeah," Blake says thoughtfully. "Maybe she found something interesting to film." I nod, and walk outside where I run into Felicity. I smile at her and continue walking, hoping to avoid her. I still don't know what to think of her now, and I feel a little bit ashamed of that. I should give her a chance, and show some understanding but it is just so hard. I hate all the crap in this world and one of the biggest things I hate are drugs. I've seen so much drug related tragedy in my time on the streets.

"Matt!" I hear Felicity's voice behind me so I turn around to face her. She walks over to me and looks into my eyes solemnly. Those beautiful eyes could get her anywhere! One look and I am already mesmerised!

"Are you okay?" She grabs my hand and steps even closer. "I think we need to have a good talk."

I nod. "Yep, we do."

We find a nice spot on the beach. The sun has only just gone down and the moon is already shining enough for us to see each other clearly. I wish it was darker though, because then it would be easier for me to speak my mind, and not be hypnotised by Felicity's stunning looks. She is still looking at me with those intensely dazzling eyes of hers. She obviously is aware of what a powerful force they are, and she certainly knows how to use them!

"Matt," she begins and clutches my hand tighter. "I don't know where to start. Can you tell me what's going on in your mind, especially after seeing my video?"

No, I don't want to say what's going on in my mind, because I don't like saying bad things! I'll just try to be reasonable, understanding and honest. Even if I may have had a crush on her before, I'm not sure what I'm feeling now, and I shouldn't let my feelings get in the way of what needs to be said.

"Felicity, I don't know how I'm feeling. I never thought you'd be the type to take drugs and especially hurt yourself. You just seem so level-headed and confident, like you know what you want in life and you're the type to go get it. Honestly, when I first met you I thought you were a snob. But after getting to know you a bit, I really began to like you... I mean, I like... You know what I mean. I thought you were sweet to everyone, especially me, and you're nice, funny, intelligent, and very pretty." That last compliment was hard to say. I had to choke it out, because I don't want her to get the wrong idea. I still don't know what I want.

"Don't get me wrong. I mean, I know you've had a tough life, as we all have, and you have your own reasons for turning to drugs, but it's just that I never usually associate with people who do drugs. I've seen what it can do—it turns people into violent criminals, who even steal from their own friends. I can't see you going that far, but I still don't understand why you would do it. I don't know if I ever will understand, no matter how hard I try."

"Oh my God." Felicity loosens her grip on my hand. "So are you saying that you don't want to be friends anymore?"

I don't know what I'm saying. I don't know what I'm feeling and I don't know how to deal with this.

"No." I choose the safest answer. "No way. I still want to be friends, for sure. But I need you to help me understand why. I'll get over it, I'm sure, but it is still a big shock for me. You're the first girl I've ever had a real crush on..." Crap! Did I just say that? I close my eyes, hoping she didn't hear it. Her grip tightens again on my hand. Fudge, she did hear!

"Really? Do you really like me like that?" Her eyes have widened even further, and she has a cheeky grin on her face. I roll my eyes knowing that I have been defeated.

"Oh come on Felicity! Every guy who's met you probably has a crush on you! Stop acting like you didn't know. You know very well how gorgeous you are, and you know that you could have any guy you wanted..."

She rushes forward and presses her tender lips against mine. Once the shock settles I kiss her back, briefly and softly, before pulling away once I realise what is happening. Struggling to hide my excitement about my first proper kiss ever, I try to look at her sternly.

"I dunno, Felicity." My heart is racing, and I try to steady my breathing. I'm all worked up and I just want to pounce her. "Not just yet. Please. I can't do it. I need more time…"

God, I can't even spit out what I'm trying to say. So I do what I always do in situations like this—run! I turn and run back to the resort, head straight up to my bedroom and jump into bed, pulling the covers up over my head like a sissy boy.

Jason: It's rumble time.

Here we are standing in a wide empty field, several kilometres south of the suburbs. My town is close-by to this semi-rural area. Most of the wheat fields have been replaced with vineyards and orchards, but there are still a few fields left, perfect for a rumble of this size. My crew has been here gearing up for an hour or so and Jono's crew just rocked up. All up there is about forty of us. If either crew is outnumbered, the extra people usually stand and watch, but they always end up joining in eventually. Let's just hope these menaces don't bring many more than us.

It is getting close to midnight, and a lot of my guys are beginning to get drunk. I hope they are still able to fight well! Most of them say that they fight better when they're drunk because they can't feel the pain as much.

It's a warm night, but I feel a cold shiver, so I shake it off immediately. I know I shouldn't be here, my gut feeling is telling me so. I should be with Kate and Kelly, but I've got to put an end to what I started. It's just a shame it may have to end here for me forever. The unwritten rules state that no weapons are to be used in rumbles, but there always are a few. A few of my guys have their switchblades with them just in case the Skinnies bring weapons. And of course, our loaded guns are hidden safely in our cars if it comes to that. I hope it doesn't come to that.

I remember the worst rumble ever to take place in this country, which was all over the news, and six people were killed with dozens more seriously injured. It happened when I was younger, before I became involved in any of this, but I remember reading about it in the paper. Apparently, two old-school gangs, the Southside Renegades and the Main Street Bangers, which have long since been dissolved, had a beef from way back. Every single time a member from each gang would bump into one another, no matter how public a place, they would start a fight, often ending in a shooting or a stabbing. The leaders of each gang decided to put an end to it, because the police were putting serious heat on, so they organised a rumble in a field similar to this one. They both agreed on no weapons, and an equal number of fighters. Both sides abided by the amount of people they brought but everyone brought a weapon of some kind. No guns were used, but the rumble turned out to be a bloodbath. Years of anger and resentment were unleashed that terrible night and it took a hundred riot police to break it up. I fear that tonight will be a repeat.

"Fire up Jason!" Tooth shakes me by the shoulders and slaps my face lightly. I return the favour and scream— "Come on!"

Moments later, the Skinnies arrive, with their Asian allies not far behind. They park their cars, mainly black four-wheel-drives, on the opposite side of the field, which is about two-hundred metres away. Each car is full, and there are ten cars, including a couple of vans, which makes about fifty to sixty of them.

This is crazy.

I can't believe we're going to go through with this. I'm secretly hoping that the cops turn up and put a stop to this before it even starts. But I know that will never happen and I know that I need to stay strong for my crew and just get this over with. Of the rumbles I've been involved with, I've seen and heard of a few ways to begin. The first and most common is for two of the best fighters to fight in the middle, and as soon as one is knocked down, everyone else charges. Often though, everyone charges as soon as the first punch is thrown. The second, which I have never seen, because it is so medieval, is similar to the first, but the two fighters who have the biggest quarrel with each other fight to the death and then everyone goes home. I've only ever heard of that happening in the gladiator era, or like on the movie Troy, but never while I've been around, thank God. The third is simply that everyone just charges one another. I don't know what's going to happen tonight, but we'll come to an agreement.

I walk towards the middle to meet the leader of the Skinnies. He is slightly taller than me and also a bit bigger. I'm not threatened though. I've beaten bigger dudes than this one. His eyes look dark and cold, which puts me off a bit.

"What's it going to be?" I state bluntly.

"Yes little fellah." He seems to beginning and snarling slightly. "This is between you and Lawrence, but seeing as he has lost his hand, thanks to your punk friend, I will be taking his place." He spits out each word with a snarl so fierce like little balls of fire.

"So we're going to fight til the first knockout?"

"Nope." He grins even wider. "We're going to fight to the death."

My heart stops.

I cannot believe my own ears. I can't back down now, because once another fighter challenges you to a duel, even to the death, it is dishonourable and cowardly to chicken out. Ridiculous I know. I nod, and run back to tell the others. He just stands there, removes his shirt, and awaits my return.

"He wants a death-duel," I almost stutter to Joseph, who begins to curse, realising the seriousness of this situation. He's always been used to fun and games, just a bit of biffo and everyone goes home alive. It's never gotten this serious before.

"Sweet!" Tooth says, and tries to pass me his switchblade. "You might need this, just take it."

I shake my head and run back out into the middle of the field to fight this massive, muscle-bound warrior.

This is it.

There's no turning back now.

CHAPTER 14

~ *Reconciled* ~

Felicity: The sun wakes me up as it shines through my window, already high in the sky. Blake has let us sleep-in for the first time since we've been here! I suppose it is a Sunday, and it is the nice thing to do. I wonder how Bec and Matt are. They both seemed to run away from me last night! I hope it wasn't something I said... Oh how embarrassing—I just remembered that I had kissed Matthew and he ran away straight after! I don't think I'm a bad kisser and it's not like I had garlic or onions for tea! Oh well, I just hope he doesn't hold it against me, or run and tell everyone about it. I don't think he will, but I don't know him that well. Who would he tell anyway? I guess I don't want him telling Blake because I'm sure he doesn't want people hooking up with each other while on his rehab program. Oh who cares, it was just one small kiss. I hope Matt doesn't think I'm a screwed-in-the-head druggy *and* a slut now!

After a nice late breakfast, or should I say brunch, I head outside and sit on a grassy hill to the right of the shack. Ha, I'm still calling this place a "shack". It's funny because you'd have to be a multi-millionaire to own this as your shack, or holiday home. There are enough rooms here for probably fifty people or more, including a couple of big dormitories which could fit fifteen beds each. Out the back are the secure wings built over a hundred years ago where we haven't been able to see inside. It's a shame not being allowed in there—it would be interesting to see, although a bit eerie too! There is a huge grassed area on one side of the quadrant surrounding the pool. Apparently that's where some buildings had burnt down— Blake hasn't told us much about it besides mentioning it in his introductory video. Maybe I'll ask him later.

We tend to hang out in the new main building out the front though because that's where our bedrooms are, and the dining room. The hall is attached to this building and extends out to the right, where it joins the grass where I am sitting. I hadn't noticed til late last week that the hall is actually a basketball court, with a stage up the front, and the basketball ring hoisted up near the ceiling when not in use. I guess I didn't notice earlier because of all the chairs and the removable carpet. It is kind of weird having this place so far away from anything else. I guess that's the idea of it—to get mentally ill people away from the distractions and temptations of life. I wonder if it has a name, this resort. I haven't even bothered to look at the signs out the front.

Matthew spots me and walks over.

"Hey there," he smiles, which surprises me. "How ya doing today?"

"Not too bad thanks." I lay back onto the grass playing it cool.

"Just sunbaking?"

"Yep."

"Cool. Are you wearing sunscreen? It's scorching out here."

"Nope."

"Oh okay. Want me to get you some?"

I decide not to tease him like I normally would. "No thanks."

Wow, what a riveting conversation. I glance over and notice that he has taken off his shirt to bask in the sun also. This is the first time I have seen all his scars and skin-grafts. I guess he's been too self-conscious about them up until now. He always seems to wear a t-shirt when swimming in the pool or the beach.

I move myself closer so that I can touch his perfect, beautiful skin lightly. He doesn't even flinch but just looks towards me longingly. I move my fingers up his soft, fragile skin, goose-bumps forming and spreading, until I reach the beginnings of his scars—I immediately notice the contrasting roughness, but it doesn't even bother me. I notice that Matthew's expression has changed to become a little more uneasy.

"It's okay," I say to him as I begin to kiss the damaged areas of his chest and stomach. I give him dozens of small, delicate kisses as I move up to his neck, wanting more but also knowing that I mustn't. I am hesitant, expecting him to push me off again. He doesn't even budge, and I reach his perfect, full lips and pause for a moment, waiting in anticipation, millimetres away from a kiss that I know will be the best one I've ever had. Even better than the last.

After the kiss, which lived up to my expectations I pull away, hoping that Matthew doesn't think I'm just playing with him. I face him and look into his sparkling big brown eyes.

"I'm sorry Matt." I hold his hand. "I couldn't resist. I really like you but I understand if you need time to figure out your own feelings. Even if you decide that just being friends is what you want then that's cool. We'll probably go our own separate ways after all this is over anyway."

He looks sincerely into my eyes and causes my heart to skip a beat or three. He looks at me seriously, almost as if he wants to push me away but somehow I think he is actually trying to fight the urge to kiss me again. He moves towards me slowly, so I close my eyes waiting for another kiss.

"Oh look, there's Rebecca," he says suddenly and shifts away from me. I open my eyes and see Rebecca wandering over to us.

Rebecca: "Hey," I state plainly to the other two who have a guilty look on their faces. They look very comfortable with each other, which I suppose is nice, but I wish I could feel the same.

"Hi Bec," Felicity says, smiling as usual. "How are ya?"

"Yeah, good thanks," I lie. I'm tired and grumpy—I spent most of the night figuring out what to film and finally got it done. Now I'm contemplating throwing out the tape or burning it so the others don't see it, but at the same time I'm glad I finished it because now

I feel much better. I never knew that just voicing my thoughts and feelings would remove such a heavy, deadly weight off my shoulders. I'm just too scared to show these guys because I'm really beginning to like them and I think they might like me too. I don't want to do anything to ruin that.

"Blake wants to know if you guys want to go waterskiing?" I ask them. "He's launching the boat now."

"Hell yes!" They both jump up excited at the sound of waterskiing. I'm not too sure about it. In fact I'm so scared that I'm nearly shitting myself just thinking about it! We wander down to where Blake and another worker are launching the boat.

"Felicity," I beckon her to come closer. "Thanks for the chat last night. It really helped." I brave a smile and she grins widely back at me.

"Anytime Bec! That's what friends are for."

I can now safely say I take back anything bad I've ever thought about Felicity. I will still have to be cautious around her for a while, to protect myself, but for now I'll just enjoy the friendship.

Blake explains a few rules, and about how to actually ski. Felicity has been skiing in the snow before so she volunteers to go first. We put our lifejackets on and set out offshore. The water is very calm today and the sun is scorching hot. I'm grateful that I put sunscreen on earlier; the others are doing so now.

"Let's do this," Felicity says, readying herself as she drops into the water. She manages to get up on the second attempt, which Blake says is very good. Blake takes the boat to the other side of the bay and back before Felicity falls off and signals that she's had enough. Matthew's turn is next. I'm trying to avoid having my turn—after seeing Felicity fall off like she did, it has put me off even more! Matthew has about four attempts before he gets up and then he stacks it soon after. On the next attempt he manages to stay on for a while. Felicity cheers at him and he shouts back. It looks like he's having lots of fun!

"Woohoo!" He shouts, putting one hand in the air and nearly losing his balance. He quickly grabs the handle with both hands and steadies himself. He falls off a couple more times and then his time is up. Oh great—my turn!

"Are you ready Rebecca?" Blake asks me, as Matthew climbs back into the boat. My face must be showing my fear because then he says, "You don't have to have a turn if you don't want to."

"Come on Bec," Felicity encourages me. "It's so much fun! And it doesn't hurt much at all when you crash."

"That's if I can even do it," I mumble as I reluctantly slide myself into the water.

"Now, remember to keep you arms straight and down, while the boat pulls you okay?"

I nod. Easier said than done! I grab the handle and the boat takes off slowly. I watch the rope as it begins to unravel, and wait endlessly for it to tighten and yank my arms out of their sockets. Suddenly, the rope becomes taut and pulls me forward so quickly that my face slaps the water. I quickly pull myself up and spit out my mouthful of salt water. Good effort Bec, I shake my head and grab the rope again.

"Good try! Have another go!" Felicity is still trying to encourage me. I don't think it'll work, but oh well.

The boat takes off again, this time I lean back further and bend my legs. I'm determined to get it right this time. Crap, the tightening rope takes me by surprise again, but this time I almost get up before falling down again.

Okay, one last time and then I'm giving up. This is so embarrassing!

Once again I pick up the rope and steady myself, Felicity calls out some encouraging words that I barely hear, and I concentrate on watching the rope as it tightens. It pulls me hard again, but this time I am ready and get up for a few seconds before losing my balance and toppling over.

Oh, screw this!

I signal to give up but Felicity shakes her head and says something to Blake. "Have another try!" She yells out to me but I shake my head. She nods and smiles, a new cheekiness in her grin. I sigh; she's too stubborn to give up. And I'm too weak to give in!

I grab the handle again and try to remember everything—arms stretched out, knees bent, lean back, and try to stay balanced once I'm up. I barely get time to run that through my mind before I realise the rope is yanking at me and I'm up, skiing across the perfectly flat water only disturbed by the boat's wake. After I manage to steady a few wobbles I get the hang of it pretty quickly and experience the newfound confidence that Matthew did moments earlier. I decide not to take any of my hands off the rope though! Felicity and Matthew are cheering at me, but I can't make out what they are saying. The water is cold on my face because of the air rushing by, which makes a nice change on a hot day. I am too busy enjoying this rush, this adrenaline-producing experience to notice that we are about to make the turn to come back. I had watched the other two do it but I'm a bit frightened. Before I know it, the boat begins to turn in a wide arc and the rope follows, pulling me with it. I try to lean in and take the corner, but it feels unnatural so I just let go of the rope, ski for several metres before sinking and falling flat on my face. Again! The boat comes by and picks me up, with everyone cheering.

"Nicely done Rebecca," Blake says, smiling, as he helps me back into the boat. Matthew pulls the rope in and we cruise the bay for a bit, Blake showing off how fast his speedboat can go! I've never had so much fun in my life! Matthew is screaming with joy, Felicity's face is beaming, and I realise I am smiling so widely that my cheeks are hurting.

Matthew: Wow. Wow! That was incredible! I've always wondered what waterskiing would be like. I always thought it would be too hard, or painful when you crashed, but it was just fun!

"Let's do it again!" I shout.

"We're going to have lunch now," Blake says, guiding the boat back to shore. "We can have another go later if you want."

We all cheer.

I breathe out a huge lungful of air, still excited about what I just did. As we approach the shore, we can see a motorbike pull up in the car park alongside the buildings. A figure that we can't quite distinguish jumps off and runs towards us, pulling off his helmet and chucking it. When he gets closer we realise that it's Jason!

"Jason!" Rebecca shouts, and begins to run towards him but hesitates. He gets to us quickly and we can see the wounds on his face. He is bleeding from a cut on his left cheek, and an even worse one from his head. His t-shirt is also torn, with what looks like a long, but shallow cut from a knife.

"Jason, are you okay?" Blake rushes over to him.

"They're after me," he says frantically. "They're coming!"

M**atthew:** Jason looks scared. The tough, hard look he usually has is gone and is replaced by the same expression I saw on my dad's face when we were running away from our home. He collapses suddenly, so Blake and I help carry him back to the sickroom, where the nurse tends to his wounds and gives him something to drink. He looks very pale, but peaceful in a way, lying there semi-conscious, not really aware of what is going on. We leave him to rest and Blake calls a meeting in the hall. He quickly explains the situation to everyone.

"Okay, so we need everyone to stay alert because although he may have said what he did in a delirious state, there may be some truth behind it. We won't bother him until he's ready to talk. And we won't call the police until we know what is happening because this is supposed to be a safe haven—no-one knows where it is and the police aren't allowed to touch you guys while you're here. However, your safety comes first and foremost so if he has gotten into some big trouble while he's been gone, then the police do have the right to arrest him. We'll keep an eye out, and Tim, you can drive to the end of Anchor Beach Road to keep watch for tonight okay? Call us over the radio if you see anything."

Tim nods and doesn't waste any time. We can all sense the urgency of the situation.

"Now, we do need a plan of action, in case Jason is right. Everyone, go to your rooms right away and get the backpacks you used for the bushwalk. Somebody grab Jason's as well." He points to the other staff. "Go get the food and equipment we were going to use for the camping trip. It looks like we'll be having our camping trip earlier than I thought."

We all jump into action and do what Blake instructed and are back in the hall within fifteen minutes. I had grabbed all of my belongings and also a few extra clothes from the communal closet, as we were told we could do. I didn't know where we were going or for how long, if at all, but I guess we've got to be prepared.

"Okay, good," Blake begins again. "Now, we need to fit all of this food into your backpacks." He points to a table which is covered in cans, packets, boxes and bottles of food and water. There were also four sleeping bags, a tent, and a couple of other smaller bags.

"In here," Blake says, referring to one of the smaller bags, "is a whole lot of camping gear that you may need. It includes fire-lighting gear, proper maps of the area, torches, cooking gear including cutlery, tools, a pair of binoculars, and a compass. You already have first-aid kits and the radios, so once you figure out how to fit all of this into your packs, you'll be set! Hopefully you won't have to camp out for long, but it's better to be prepared for anything. Good luck!"

Yeah, looks like we'll need it! We're going to struggle to fit only the food into our backpacks, let alone all the other stuff. Blake gave a few hints, such as using the straps to attach our sleeping bags on the outside to save space. We manage to fit all the food and drink in but had to rearrange several times to fit the extra items in. Finally, when we thought we had finished, we realised that the tent was still sitting on the table, and our backpacks were bulging enough already. We decide that it is warm enough to sleep outside so we leave the tent here. As we finish up and Blake is explaining the plan, Jason stumbles into the room. We all stop to ask him how he is.

"Hey man," I say and put my hand on his shoulder. He still looks paler than the moon was last night. "How ya doin' now?"

"Better, thanks." He braves a smile. "I need a good feed though."

I laugh and the girls rush off to find him some food from the kitchen. They arrive moments later with two huge chicken and salad rolls, and a can of soft-drink.

"Thanks girls." He smiles at them and tucks into his food. Blake continues to give us more instructions on where to go and what to do in certain situations. Jason looks at us intrigued for a moment before eating some more. Even once Blake had finished I am still trying to force the zipper up on my very full backpack. Just as I manage to get It up by putting my weight on the pack to squeeze that extra bit of room, one of the office staff comes bursting into the hall.

"They're coming!"

CHAPTER 15

~ In The Face Of Adversity ~

Jason: Bloody hell. I didn't even get to finish my second roll! I'll take it with me, wherever we're going.

"Tim called on the radio," the office lady continues frantically. "They're not far off, and they shot out his tyres to stop and check his vehicle."

Everyone is motionless, with terrified expressions on their faces.

"What's happening guys?" I ask them.

"You tell us," Felicity snaps.

"We've got to get you to safety," Blake replies. "You might have to camp out for a couple of nights until it's safe. Geoff will take the four-wheel-drive up the track to the north as a diversion, while you guys head south through the sand-dunes for a couple of clicks until you reach the bushland. Head inland from there and find a safe and secluded spot. There are maps to the nearest town, Port Dowie, if you feel you need to get somewhere public, although it's at least two days walk. I'll call you on your radio once it is safe okay?"

Everyone nods and grabs their backpacks.

"Why don't we just take the boat?" Matthew asks. "They won't be able to follow us."

"No, it'll take too long to launch it again."

"They've got a sniper rifle, they'll just pick us off," I say bluntly.

"What?! What do you mean...?"

"I'll explain later!" I recognise the urgency although the others don't seem to get it. I need to be stern and strong again. "We've gotta go. Now!"

I finish my can of drink while we get a move on outside. Geoff begins to drive up the off-road track to create a diversion. As we head down the beach I glance at the road briefly and recognise the black four-wheel-drives in the distance, speeding along towards the compound. We disappear into the sand dunes, in case they check the beach, but stay parallel to the water for a while until we hit the densest bushland. Before we head inland I have a quick peek with the binoculars at the resort. I can see three black four-wheel-drives parked, and another racing off to chase Geoff down the track. I cannot see any of the thugs but they're probably already searching the buildings.

God I hope they don't hurt Blake.

I turn to follow the others, who are already walking briskly inland.

"We've gotta get a move on," I say, gasping for breath, while jogging past the others. It won't be long until the gang realises we've gone and begins the hunt. Bloody hell, this is my entire fault, and I've put these guys' lives in danger. What was I thinking?! Looking at their faces now though, I can see a new braveness and courage that has replaced the once terrified and gloomy appearance. They could've easily just sent me off on my own to hide, but they chose to come with me. Well, Blake probably insisted, which seems more likely, but they could've refused and said it was my problem and for me to deal with it on my own. I'm glad I've got these guys. They're my only friends now. They're the ones keeping me going. I've been running away from these hoods all night and morning, and I'm feeling so exhausted that if I just saw a picture of a bed I would fall into a deep sleep.

Stay focussed!

Matthew overtakes me and sets a faster pace, which I am determined to match. I glance behind and am glad to see that the girls are keeping up as well. We've got to keep going at this pace for at least another few hours until we find a nice hiding spot for the night. Night-time will be a lot harder to walk this quickly without falling over rocks and logs. But it will also be harder for them to find us. We've agreed not to use the torches unless necessary because anyone following us will be able to spot it easily.

None of us has spoken for this entire trip besides when I stumbled and Felicity asked if I was okay. I think we're just eager to get to our destination, wherever that may be.

Finally, when I am beyond exhaustion Matthew guides us through a tight, naturally-made tunnel of shrubs, trees and bushes. It is off the main track and is hard to notice because it is so overgrown. We have to bend down a lot to fit through and it leads into a small clearing, large enough to set up our sleeping bags. Directly behind is a huge rock ridge, about fifteen metres high, which steadily climbs higher the further it goes along, probably joining to a mountain or hill of some sort. It is hard to see very far because of all the trees and undergrowth around the clearing. I drop my backpack and collapse on the mossy ground—my head spins and my vision blurs until I fall asleep within seconds.

Felicity: "Geez, look at Jason!" I point to him as he passes out on the ground as soon as we enter the clearing. "He must be tired!"

Matthew rolls his eyes and wanders back through the tunnel with the binoculars. I pull out a blow-up pillow, inflate it and place it under Jason's head. I wonder what he did to make all those people chase him. And I wonder why he came back to us. I thought he hated this place and that's why he escaped! I hope he tells us what happened, although he is very secretive, so I doubt he will.

"I'm starving," I say to Rebecca, who is resting up against her backpack. "Want a muesli bar?"

She nods so I toss her one before grabbing my own. It is nearly sundown already—we walked for quite a few hours.

"My legs are killing me!" I flop down next to Rebecca.

"Yeah, same here." Rebecca closes her eyes to have a nap, so I do the same.

"Wake up Felicity." I am awoken by Matthew giving me a light tap on my shoulder. I sit bolt upright sensing that something is wrong. The other two are both awake as well.

"What's wrong?" I ask urgently.

"Hey?" He looks surprised. "Oh, nothing. Tea's ready!"

"Oh, good," I reply, referring to tea being ready as well as the fact that nothing is wrong. It is dark now and Matthew has set up our sleeping area in the most secluded corner of the clearing, and he is now cooking our tea on the tiny portable gas stove. It is baked beans, sausages, bread and canned vegetables. I initially screw my nose up at the sight and smell of our meal, but then my hunger gets the better of me and I gulp it down quicker than anyone else.

"We can't light a fire can we?" Rebecca asks.

"Nope." Matthew doesn't even look up from his food. "It'll attract our hunters, if they're still following, with the smell and the light. Also, I heard Blake say that it's illegal during summer to have a campfire in any National Park due to bushfire risk."

"Fair enough. But then it's not real camping is it?"

"And I guess the fire-lighting stuff was pretty useless then?" I ask dryly.

"Yeah, but it did help to light the gas stove, which is a lot more contained than a fire," Matthew says, mimicking my sarcasm.

"Thanks guys," Jason breaks his silence. "You didn't have to do this you know."

"Yeah, but we wanted to," Matthew says sincerely. "We're supposed to work as a team remember? And you're still part of this group!"

Jason smiles for the first time since he got back. I don't recall him smiling very often, if at all, so it is a nice change.

"So what happened?" Asks quiet little Rebecca. I was hoping someone would ask that.

"It's a long story." Jason puts his empty plate down and looks indifferent.

"Go on then," I say after a moment's silence. "We've got all night."

"Okay, I'll try to give you the short version but I might get carried away. We've gotta keep an ear out too. Anyway, I escaped on the bus, as you know, and when I got home not much had changed. My flatmate, Jimmy, told me that our rival crew were after my blood as revenge for many terrible things that I had done to them. Well it wasn't all me, but anyway, they mainly wanted *me* because I am the leader of my crew. So I did what's normal for such situations and set a date for a rumble—it was to be the rumble to settle all vendettas between our crews and I set it for midnight last night. A couple of days ago I went to visit my baby and ex-girlfriend, and pretty much fell in love again. I knew the right thing to do was to quit the gang and look after my girls, but I also knew that it would be a death-sentence if I did betray my crew like that. I knew that the only way was to go ahead with the rumble and hopefully come out alive with no more debts to be paid."

Jason picks up a stick and starts snapping it into little pieces, while gathering his thoughts, which are obviously going at a million miles an hour.

"On the night of the rumble," Jason continues, trying to keep his voice down, "we arrived an hour early to check out the field. We chose the side that was slightly uphill so we could get better momentum. I counted forty-one on my side. When the Skinnies rocked up, they outnumbered us, but we weren't scared because we had more well-built and experienced lads than they did. The leader of the Skinnies came forward, and so did I. This is when things started to turn bad… The Skinny asked me for a death-duel, and make no mistake, this dude was huge—bigger than me! My mate Tooth tried to give me a switchblade but I refused. I wanted a fair, clean fight. The Skinny had other ideas. One of my mates had shot this Skinny's best friend earlier that week, so he was out for revenge—on top of all the other things they wanted me for. So when he challenged me to a death-duel, he meant it…"

"What do you mean by death-duel?" I innocently ask Jason, and immediately figure out the answer myself.

"Just like it says Felicity. A fight to the death. Anyway, we paced in a circle in the middle of the field until he lunged at me and I dodged him. We exchanged several blows, many of which would kill the average person. I managed to duck and weave several times until he got me in a bear-hold—his vice-like grip felt like it was crushing every bone in my body. I felt myself fading, and my eyes went all blurry, but I forced myself to get one more head-butt in. I broke his nose with my forehead and he stumbled back. While this was happening, all of the remaining crewmembers from both sides had charged one another and were fighting fiercely. I glanced over at one stage and saw Joseph on the ground, being kicked in the head and body by two Skinnies, so I left the guy I was fighting to go help him.

I knocked out both Skinnies in seconds.

Before I could even turn around though, I was grabbed from behind and pulled to the ground—the monster was still trying to wrestle with me! I struggled out of his grip again and jumped up, putting my fists up to challenge him to a proper boxing match. He followed suit, laughing while he pulled out a knife, and begun to swing wildly at me again. I knew a guy of this size would tire quickly, I was hoping, so I dodged stray punches and the knife's sharp edge for a while, although he managed to nick me a couple of times." Jason points to his cuts.

"Finally I found the perfect opportunity for a powerful uppercut. You could hear his jaw shatter over all the noise from the ninety-odd men fighting. He fell like a ton of bricks, and he wasn't getting back up. I looked around to see if the others had seen, and they had. I've never seen anything like it in my life.

If you can imagine nearly one hundred guys fighting one another, throwing punches, kicks, wrestling moves, screaming, swearing, and all the blood and mess that comes with it, then that's only the beginning of what I saw that night. It was a battlefield. And a very chaotic one."

Jason turns away briefly and shakes his head. I've never seen him talk so excitedly but nervously about something.

"Once everyone had seen that I had knocked this guy out, they all stopped fighting and formed a massive circle around us. The Skinnies knew that their friend was about to die—he was the one who had challenged me to a death-duel so it would be even worse for him to back out now. He had regained consciousness and was kneeling, dazed, and waiting for me to finish him off… Someone from Jono's crew passed me a huge twelve inch blade. Everyone stood in silence, waiting for my move. This would be the end to all of our fights, all of our beefs, and all of our troubles. The Skinnies and the Asian gangs would stay out of our territory for good, and we would leave them alone too. Why couldn't we have just come to an agreement like this without fighting? I don't know, but I do know what happened next. And I still cannot believe it."

He clutches his chest, and listens intently as if he heard someone coming, after realising that his voice had gained quite a bit of volume.

"I stepped forward, in front of the guy. He looked up at me, pleading for me not to do it. He even whispered that he had a baby son. But I had to do it. There were ninety-odd guys there who knew I had to do it. They would kill me in an instant if I didn't. It was either me or him. But I turned away. I walked away from him to signal the end of the battle, the end of the war. My crew moved to follow me, but then Paul from Jono's crew shouted—'I'll bloody do it then!' He ran at the guy with a huge, sharp machete, in an attempt to chop his head off. I didn't have time to think—my mind went blank, but my body just moved quicker than it ever has before. I ran at Paul and tackled him to the ground just millimetres before he reached the Skinny."

Jason is breathing heavily.

"Paul landed on his blade, which sliced easily into his abdomen. I dunno if he survived, I doubt it because they would've been too scared and stupid to take him to the hospital. Instead they chased me.

'You're a dead man Jason! You bloody traitor!' I heard Jono yell as I stood there stunned. It didn't even register to me until later that the Skinny I had saved actually thanked me. The Skinnies bolted, with Jono's crew in hot pursuit. Most of Jono's crew had walked or rode their motorbikes to the field, and only had a couple of cars. They pulled out guns from nowhere and shot at the Skinnies who decided it was safer to run into the vineyards than head back to their cars. So Jono's crew stole their four-wheel-drives. I had already started bolting towards the vineyards, with my crew in tail, bullets whizzing by us. Just before we reached the first row of vines I looked over towards Jono's car and saw him pulling out a sniper rifle from the boot. He didn't waste time in loading it and pointed it straight at me. I dove into the first row just as the bullet whizzed past my head. These guys are maniacs, and I knew that. But I didn't realise they would turn against me so quickly. I was just grateful that my crew was being so loyal. I guess I've done a lot for them in the past.

We ran and ran, ducking and weaving between rows of vines, with the four-wheel-drives chasing us down. They couldn't keep up though, because once they committed to a row, we could duck through the vines to get away and they had to drive to the end before they could try and reach us again. A few of them decided to chase us on foot. Joseph and Tooth's guns slowed them down a bit. Eventually we made it back to the suburbs and I told the others to get somewhere safe and not to worry about me. So they ran one way and I ran the other. Jono's crew emerged soon after and it's pretty obvious who they followed. I kept running until I spotted a motorbike at a set of traffic lights. I pulled the rider off without hesitation, apologised—which, for the record, is something I never used to do. I then rode all the way here. I got a fair distance from them and tried to hide a few times, even by stopping in a couple of small towns to help myself to some free petrol—which I think helped them catch up. But no matter what I did, they still managed to follow. So here I am."

He sighs heavily and looks at us for a response. I am totally speechless—this guy is dangerous. And he has put us all in danger, which I personally think is so selfish. But like Matt said before, we're in this together as a team, so I'll stick with that philosophy.

"Whoa," I try to say genuinely. "That is crazy Jason! Are you going to be okay?"

"Yeah." He nods. "I think so."

Matthew walks over to him and puts his arm around his shoulder. "You're safe now champ."

Jason nods, looking a bit on edge.

"Will they give up looking for you?" Rebecca asks.

"No. Maybe. I'm not sure. While they're still in the heat of the moment they'll probably split up and attempt to search this National Park, but then they'll give up and go home and wait for me. I just hope they don't try to get Kate and Kelly. Cos then I'd really have to kill them!"

My eyes dart to the ground after that comment. I'm not sure if he's joking now or being serious. He's said he'd never kill anyone, but who knows what he's capable of. It makes me uncomfortable hearing him say something like that.

Matthew: Far out, Jason's been to hell and back! I wonder why, of all the places he could run to, he came back here. Oh well, it doesn't matter now. All that matters is that he's safe and we're all here for him.

"Do you think we should have someone on lookout in case they're nearby?"

"Yeh, we should take it in turns."

"I'll go first." Felicity quickly volunteers and heads off back through the tunnel to find a good position. I think she just needed to get away for a while after hearing Jason's story. It didn't look like she reacted too well to it. She kept gripping my arm tighter and tighter til it hurt! We all need time to let it sink in I guess. Rebecca has gone quiet again, unsure of what to do or say and I'm pretty much the same. We're just not used to being in such a dangerous situation, unprepared and unsure of what will happen next. I mean, I've been in dangerous situations before, probably even worse, but I'm not sure about these girls. Being on my own for so long I have

learnt how to fend for myself—find food, water, and shelter, but I
don't know if I can protect myself and the others from a bullet. And
I don't think Jason is in any state to help protect us either. After he
finished his story, he just gazed into space for a few moments, fury
mixed with fear in his eyes, before going back to sleep. I wonder if
these guys really do have guns. Maybe there's another way we can
confront them. I guess I'll discuss it with the others in the morning.
Rebecca wanders over and sits next to me. I look at her and smile.

"How ya doing Bec?"

She smiles and shrugs. "I dunno. I guess we've all got a lot on
our minds, and now this, but I'm burning inside. I'm aching to tell
all of you my story. I want to show you my video. It's like a huge
weight on my shoulders and I know I'll feel much better once I've
told you. I felt a whole lot better after telling you some of my story
briefly the other day, but that relief didn't last long. It was like the
tip of the iceberg what I told you and I feel like I will go down like
the *Titanic* very soon if I can't get it all out in the open. I hope this
isn't selfish of me, is it? I mean, Jason's obviously the one who we're
helping at the moment and I feel guilty that I need to share my past
with you guys and take your attention away from him."

"Rebecca, don't be silly! Of course it's not selfish! We've all had
a chance to share our stories, our pasts, and our secrets with one
another, and now it's your turn. I don't know if right at this moment
is the best time though, because we're all be a bit preoccupied, but as
soon as this is over you'll have our undivided attention okay?"

I take her hand, holding it tight, and she smiles weakly and
nods. After a little while she gets up and puts Jason's sleeping bag
around him and heads off on her own to sleep. I follow, as I am
feeling exhausted and it doesn't take long for me to fall asleep.

"...Come in, over... This is Blake, over..."

The radio next to my head buzzes to life and wakes me up. I grab
it in a flash and press the transmit button.

"This is Matthew, reading you loud and clear, over..."

*"...We managed to convince them that you guys have gone home,
so they've gone. You're safe. What is your location and we'll come join*

you for the camping trip? Stay where you are, we'll come at daybreak... Over..."

"Okay we're near a ridge on the southern side of the river..."

Jason appears out of nowhere and snatches the radio from me.

"Nice try Jono," he says into the mouthpiece. "I'd recognise your wanky voice anywhere."

There is a pause.

"*...Ahh Jason. You can't run away from us forever. We will get you...*"

Jason looks at me with the same look he had when talking about his family. A look of determination. A look of rage.

"*We will find you...*"

"You won't have to... I'm coming to you."

Jason whispers something into the mouthpiece that I can't quite make out.

"Come alone."

He switches the radio off and throws it down. He gives me a few instructions before walking away.

"Wha... Jason," I try to get his attention by grabbing his arm. He pushes my hand away, stops and looks at me slowly. "What do you mean?"

"I'm going to face them. It's the only way. They won't stop searching, they won't rest until I'm dead!"

"They've got guns, they'll shoot you down on sight."

"So be it."

I grab his arm again. "I won't let you do it."

Jason's eyes look tired but determined.

"There's nothing you can say or do to stop me."

He clasps my wrist tightly, almost crushing it, and removes my hand from his arm. He gives me one more stern look to show how serious he is and then walks off without another moment's hesitation.

"Jason!"

He ignores me and disappears through the bush tunnel.

Damn it! Why does he have to be so stubborn?!

"What's going on?" Rebecca has woken up from all the commotion.

Seconds later, Felicity comes running into the clearing.

"Where's Jason going?" Felicity asks. "He wouldn't answer me when he ran past so I figured something was up."

"He's going back to face the gang. I tried to stop him."

"Oh my God," Bec begins. "What should we do?"

"What can we do?"

"We've gotta do something for goodness sake!"

"We can't!" I try to explain to the girls. "Jason's got a plan."

Jason: Man I cannot wait til this is over. It isn't exactly the ideal ending I had in mind but shit happens. At least I finally have a chance to redeem myself. I never felt completely satisfied with the way I avenged my family's murders. I mean, it felt good being able to let my anger out by beating the culprits to a pulp, but I still felt bad for not being there for them. It is something I tried to substitute by being the leader of my gang and looking after them in any way possible. I've made some close friends because of my loyalty, even if leading a thug-life is risky. But it still never felt the same as true family. We aren't blood, and blood relatives look after one another no matter what, with no expectation of return. My gang are only loyal if I do the right thing by them. It's just the way it works. If I crossed any of them, they wouldn't hesitate to take me down. Just like Jono is doing now.

With Matthew, Felicity and Rebecca it feels different. I can't explain it and it'll just piss me off if you ask, but they feel more like a true family to me.

This is why I'm sacrificing myself today for them.

I finally have the chance to do what I should've done all those years ago. I should've been home with my family that Saturday night rather than out partying with mates. But no longer do I have to let this guilt eat away at me.

I know Jono would happily kill the others too, hence why I'm going alone. It is my problem, not theirs. Even if they are family now. I'm sure they'll understand down the track. They'll look back and realise why I did this.

I couldn't say any of this aloud to Matty before I left. I couldn't give him any reason to try and stop me or follow me. I know he'll look after the girls, and I'm sure they'll look after him. I don't have to worry anymore.

My only regret is not being able to see Kelly grow up. It's funny when you think about it. I have this persona of being the toughest, meanest thug—and I am, but when it comes to my little baby girl, my heart just melts. I guess it's good that I can still feel some emotion other than anger and resentment. I'm taking this bullet for Kate and Kelly too.

It's the only way and I know that.

I can't blame Jono for wanting to hunt me down. I would've done exactly the same had it been my best mate killed. The only difference is I wouldn't kill for revenge.

I slow my run to a jog as the sand-dunes come into sight. The sunrise is magnificent.

I reach the top of the dune and look down at the beach where I told Jono to meet me. He is standing by the shore alone. I spot a few of his buddies further up the beach atop a sand-dune, keeping a watchful eye. One of them no doubt has the sniper rifle.

I approach Jono with caution, bracing for the bullet, which I hope will be quick and painless.

"Jason," Jono calls out before I reach him. "I thought you weren't going to show."

"I'm a man of my word."

"I know. That's your best trait and your biggest downfall."

"Let's just get this over with."

"Easy Jason. Relax for a minute man. Enjoy the sunrise, seeing as it will be your last."

I look out towards the sunrise. It is beautiful. My mind is clear. I can almost see my family again.

"Pity about your friends," Jono scoffs. "You shouldn't have got them involved in this."

"What friends?" I try to bluff him. "What are you talking about?"

"Blake told us all about your little friends."

No, Blake wouldn't have done such a thing. He couldn't have.

"My men should be close to finding them now. The dogs were a good investment."

My heart sinks. He tricked me. No wonder he hasn't killed me yet, he wants to torture me first by making me watch my friends die.

Not going to happen.

I close my eyes briefly and take a deep breath.

Then I charge.

I send Jono flying with a kick to the stomach and then dive to my right knowing that a bullet will be heading my way real soon. I roll away from the trail of bullets hitting the sand near me, jump up and bolt to the dunes, hoping my luck is still with me. I make it into the safety of the dunes before feeling a sting on my left arm. A bullet had grazed it.

No time to worry about a little graze. I can't believe I fell for Jono's trick! So bloody stupid. I guess my so called plan failed.

No time to worry about that either. I run faster than ever and head towards the river, hoping to find the dogs and throw them off their trail. I can't let another family be killed. I won't let it happen.

Never again.

CHAPTER 16

~ Ultimatum ~

Rebecca: This is crazy, this is insane. We are running through thick bushland at top speed, not stopping or slowing down when we've been whipped in the face, or hesitating when we come to a steep embankment. We've been running for goodness knows how long, but I know as soon as we stop I'm going to collapse. The sun is hot, and my shirt is soaked in sweat. We are suddenly stopped by a creek, which is too wide for us to jump across.

"Come on!" Matthew beckons at us and I hesitate. "We need to throw off our scent for the dogs!"

I almost forgot about those blasted animals following us, and as soon as he reminds me I can hear their barking in the distance, getting closer by the second.

We had finally convinced Matthew to let us follow Jason but lost him almost straight away and if it weren't for the barking dogs we would've run straight into the gang.

What else to do in a situation like this? Outnumbered, no weapons to fight back, and dogs to sniff us out. What else could we do but run? Matt wanted to stay and fight, or try to talk them out of killing us but Felicity told him to be sensible. These guys obviously want us dead so what's the point in talking. We heard them fire off some rounds not long ago, hopefully randomly and not because they've spotted us.

Now we've hit a creek.

There's no time to take our shoes off so we run straight into the cold water and head upstream. I trust that Matthew knows what he is doing. He starts running up and down the opposite embankment to make several scuff marks in the mud. Then he jumps from the scrub into the water, making a large splash. Ignoring the fact that he just made us sopping wet from head to toe we move as fast as we can, wading through the water. Eventually we reach a waterfall and Matthew leads us out of the water, on the same side that we went in.

"It'll throw them off," he says briefly as if to answer the question we were thinking.

He heads up a narrow, natural rock path that leads to the top of the waterfall. We barely even get a chance to admire the beauty of this scenery. I cannot hear the barking anymore, which is a relief, but we still can't stop. Matt leads us for another hour or two, only stopping briefly for a drink from our flasks, which we then refilled with creek water. I really don't know if Matthew has any clue where he is going. He hasn't even looked at the compass or map since this morning—I'm too tired to argue and I guess Felicity is too.

We eventually come to a vehicle track—a rough, rocky, dirt track which leads steeply uphill.

"Keep to the scrub," Matthew says and leads us uphill, adjacent to the vehicle track. I glance back down the hill and realise what he means. Anyone looking in the right direction with a good pair of binoculars would be able to spot us easily if we were walking directly on the dirt track. There isn't as much scrub around here for protection, but enough to serve our purpose.

It takes us about another half hour to reach the top but we make it and I think we all immediately recognise where we are. Felicity runs over and flops down onto the grass patch next to where we placed our rocks from our first trek. Blake said he'd bring us back here for a picnic.

Matt and I collapse next to Felicity and catch our breath. Everyone is too tired to even complain about soggy shoes and socks.

The sun has become swelteringly hot though so they'll dry out soon. I just realise when I look at Matt that he had carried the backpack the entire way and didn't even complain! He pulls out a big lunchbox and passes it around. We all grab a couple of sandwiches and eat them in silence. I don't want to waste my energy with conversation and I think the others feel the same. Plus we must all be listening for the dogs.

After we all practically inhale the first course, Matt passes us some fruit and the drink bottles.

"What now?" Felicity asks him. I can see that Matt is enjoying being the leader.

"We dunno if they've caught onto our trail again or not so we've just got to keep going. Hopefully they're not smart enough to split up. From here, I think we can figure out a way back home."

That last word, when he said that, I knew that's how he felt. Because I realised straight away that's how I feel. It *is* home. I don't think I've ever felt quite at home anywhere else besides the rehab clinic. It's a fantastic location, with great facilities, my own room, lots of freedom, as much food as we want, and people who care about us, about me. I've never had any of this before and I also realise that these two people, and Jason, who a few weeks ago I didn't even want to know, are now my best friends. They're my family. And I'm not going to let a gang of stupid thugs take them away from me!

"Let's do it then!" I jump up. "We can make it back there, back home. Let's show them what we're made of."

I sound more positive and enthusiastic than ever before and the others certainly pick up on this because they stand up straight away.

"I'll just have a quick look to see if they're following," Matthew says and disappears back towards the dirt track.

"You okay?" I ask Felicity.

"Yep, sweet thanks. I've never been in a mess like this before. It's scary but strangely exciting!"

"You freak," I joke with her.

Matthew sprints back over to us full-pelt.

"They're at the bottom of the dirt track heading our way!"

We jump into action. Matt grabs the back pack again and we sprint to the opposite side of the clearing. It took us half an hour to climb the dirt track to here so that means we have that amount of time as a head-start. We keep on running until we come to a skidding halt at the top of the infamous cliff.

"Oh God." Felicity sighs. "Not this again!"

"It'll be easier going down it," Matthew tries to convince her.

"We've got no ropes this time."

"Fudge."

We stare down the steep, sheer drop into the canopy of thousands of trees. God, it looks even higher than I remembered! Oh well, someone's got to make a move. I find the easiest part to sit on the edge and lower my legs over, dangling them until I can find a hand-hold, inching myself forward, knowing that one tiny slip and it'll all be over. Seconds later, that tiny slip does occur and my heart flutters wildly in response to the sudden adrenaline rush. I grip onto whatever I can and lower myself down, foot by foot. I make sure that I am always holding onto something solid before lowering myself and finding another hand-hold and another foot-hold. Felicity and Matthew are looking over the edge giving me advice, which is not helpful at all but I can't spare any energy to tell them to shut-up. Felicity begins her descent, only metres above me and she tries to follow the same path that I chose.

"Hurry girls! They're close!" Matthew says anxiously. I can hear the dogs barking—they sound vicious, hungry for our blood. I realise that we're taking far too long to climb down. It is extremely slow going, but there's no other option.

"I'm gonna find a different path down." Matt scurries off to the left to find another spot where he can climb down, rather than waiting for this easier path to become available. I am too busy looking at what he's doing to notice that Felicity's foot is coming down onto my only supporting hand—she hasn't even noticed either!

The pain causes me to let go and I fall.

Matthew: I look over just as Rebecca begins to fall, and Felicity looks like she has lost her footing and is sliding down, trying to claw at the cliff to slow her fall. Luckily they are practically halfway down and both of them land on a tiny ledge. After brushing themselves off they waste no time in climbing the rest of the way down. They stare up at me, beckoning me to hurry. The dogs sound like they are on top of us!

They are.

I look up and see two dogs come to a skidding stop at the top of the cliff, off to my right. One of them doesn't stop in time and skids right off the edge of the cliff! It tumbles down, bumping each ledge on its way before landing in a bush. It tries to get back up but is obviously too injured so just lays there. The dog at the top sees the others down the bottom and starts barking at them, even more ferociously this time. It looks agitated and is edging closer, as if it wants to jump down. Do it! Another dog joins it moments later, and almost on cue, a few of Jono's crew peer over the edge and immediately spot the others. They haven't seen me yet as I am hidden off to the left, and behind some protruding rocks. I drop myself down to the ground just as they start shooting at my friends. I look over and see the girls scattering in different directions.

"Hey! Pick on someone your own size!" I shout at the attackers to distract them. They stop shooting briefly and then naturally take aim at me instead!

I bolt into the bushland and am instantly hidden by the vast canopy of leaves. They continue spraying the trees and dozens more bullets scatter through the foliage before they realise it is pointless.

This isn't good.

We had a good half-hour lead on them and they've managed to catch up! We shouldn't have dawdled on that cliff. Hopefully they'll take just as long.

We must keep going.

Mustn't give up.

Not now. Not ever.

I don't know what it is, but the thrill of the chase is just giving us the energy to keep going. Fight or flight reaction I guess—I read about it somewhere. As long as they don't hurt the girls I don't mind what happens.

So we keep on running.

We run and run until we can't run anymore and have to stop.

"This is crazy," Rebecca says between laboured breaths. "We can't keep running."

"Yeah, this is stupid," Felicity says, looking completely exhausted.

"We have to girls. We have to keep going!" I'm beginning to get frustrated and start yelling. "We can't give up now. What else can we do?"

"I think I can answer that question."

We look up to see Jason jogging towards us.

"Jason!" The girls and I jump up.

"Hey everyone." He catches his breath for a moment. "Things didn't quite go as planned, but I guess they never do... I tried to get them to follow me—I guess you heard them shooting at me earlier... Come on, gotta keep movin'. This way."

Jason leads us to the river, and finds a cave along the embankment.

"I noticed it the other week when we were on our trek."

It is small, but well hidden with lots of trees and bushes around the top and sides, and we have to walk through the river to access it, which will hopefully trick the dogs. We all collapse in a heap.

After a few minutes of rest, I peer out the entrance to try and hear or see them coming. Jason joins me.

"Hey champ," he begins.

I continue to listen intently for danger.

"I'm sorry for everything." There is a deep sincerity in his eyes.

I look at him and smile. "It's okay Jason, I understand."

Jason: That's when I broke down. This nice, black man is far too forgiving for me to understand. I don't know how he's put up with all the abuse I've given him without wanting to bash my head in. I guess I wanted him to retaliate in order to give me an excuse to bash *him* up. Now I recognise that the anger and hatred

I've let build inside of me over these years has been so destructive that it's spilt out to all those around me. I've put my own life in danger, but even worse, I've put the lives of Kate and Kelly, my crewmembers, and my friends here in danger. But I guess it goes to show who your true friends are when in you're in such peril. Where are my crewmembers? They've been there for me before when I've been in trouble, and even saved my life on numerous occasions, but this time it's different. I need them more than ever and they're not here. Maybe they're scared of being killed or being caught by the police, or maybe they don't even know where I am. Whatever it is, true friends would look past those facts, no matter how dramatic the consequences. Friends like these people here with me now. God, I can't believe I am actually finally calling them my *friends*! My *family*!

"Matt, come here mate," I beckon for him to come back into the cave. I don't know if I've ever properly cried before but I think the tears streaming down my face now are from the many years of pain, anger and resentment. I'm actually a little embarrassed by it but for once I don't give a shit.

"I just want to thank all of you for doing this for me. You guys are braver, more courageous, and more loyal than anyone I've ever met. You've been great friends to me and I'll never forget that. But right now I've got a decision to make. Well I've actually already made it, but anyway. I'm giving myself up, again..."

"No way," Felicity objects.

"Felicity, it's okay. I've made up my mind. If I give myself up, then hopefully I can save you guys."

"It didn't work before dude," Matthew points out.

"Yeah I know, but I didn't count on Jono sending his blokes to hunt you guys. You should be safe here, if I go now."

"You can't." Rebecca begins to sob. "Please."

"I can, and I will, and only because I like you guys. If I didn't care about you I would sit back and wait here until they find us and turn this into our grave."

"Maybe they won't find us! Maybe they'll give up and go home!"

"They won't give up until I'm dead. And they won't care if you guys get killed as well. So promise me you'll stay here. No matter what, ok? Promise?"

They all eventually agree.

Time is ticking.

I get up and head to the entrance of the cave. Rebecca runs up and wraps her arms around me.

"Take care okay?" I stroke her hair gently before peeling her off me.

I walk out into the open and wade downstream a couple of hundred metres before climbing up the embankment into the shrubbery. I walk along through the thick scrub until I reach the clearing where we had lunch on our first hike. I sit on one of the rocks and wait.

It doesn't take long for the sound of barking to get closer and closer. I just sit there in silence, waiting for it to happen. Will it be a bullet from a distance or will they set their dogs onto me or maybe they'll do it point-blank, to rub it in my face that I've failed.

The shouting gets louder and more urgent, and I realise that they've spotted me. They're trying to find an easy way across the river without getting too wet. I shake my head. Cowards.

I close my eyes. I don't want to watch.

Jono looms menacingly above me and I can feel the dogs tearing at my shoes, their handlers finding it hard to keep them under control. Eventually the dogs are pulled back and I can focus on what Jono is saying to me, even though everything else is a blur. He is calling me every swearword I have ever heard. Good vocabulary, for a scumbag.

"Nice to see you too Jono," I say dryly.

"What were you thinking? Did you actually think you could get away from me? Not only did you betray your own kind and kill one of my closest friends, but you made us trek all day through this blasted forest!"

"You look worn out," I scoff.

"Don't get cheeky with me boyo. You're going to pay for what you did Jason. Fark, you have *no* idea what you're in for. I had a clean shot at you just before with this." He points to the sniper rifle slung over his shoulder. "But I didn't because I want you to suffer."

More like because he's just as bad aim as his buddies.

"You will feel more pain than you have ever felt before until you will be begging, *begging* for a bullet."

Jono pauses to take a final drag on his cigarette before putting it out on my neck. I don't even flinch. I don't want to give him the satisfaction of knowing how much it hurts.

"Yeah, you act tough there Jason." Jono screws up his face. "One last chance to show just how tough you are. I can't believe I actually let my crew back you up! I thought you were honourable enough to know the rules of a rumble, and I especially didn't think you were dumb enough to be a traitor. You for one should know how we deal with traitors…"

"Oh shut your face Jono. You're a worthless piece of trash and you dribble a whole lot of shit so like I said before, let's just get this over with." I emphasise the last part of that sentence impatiently.

I look at him with my most fearless and lethal gaze. Anyone who knows me understands that gaze means I won't go down without a fight so Jono takes a couple of steps back. I jump up and he points his gun at me.

"Do it!" I shout at him. "Just do it already! What are you waiting for?! Come on you bloody pussy, haven't you got the balls?!"

Jono's eyes light up with a mix of rage and fear. I doubt he's ever actually killed anyone. He usually gets his crewmembers to do his dirty work. His snarl turns into a snigger when he hears the sound of the other dog heading this way.

"Now you can watch your friends die."

My heart sinks as I turn to see my friends being led by Jono's men towards us. Jono signals at two of his men, who train their guns towards my friends.

Nothing is going right today.

"Target practice," Jono states coldly.

The other men dive to the ground, obviously aware of what is about to happen. My friends stop cold, not sure of what to do. These armed men, who have been guiding the three towards us, have just suddenly flattened themselves onto the ground.

"Get down!!!" I shout at the top of my lungs and my friends register just in time as the first bullets fly dangerously close to them. I waste no time and dive at Jono, pushing his gun away just as it fires. My other hand wraps tightly around his neck as we fall to the ground. His gun fires a few more times before my grip is so tight around his wrist that he is forced to let go. I make sure that his head hits the ground hard and ram it into the dirt. He's a big boy though and won't give up easily. That's fine by me. He shoves me off with his free hand and kicks desperately with his feet. I jump up and land hard on his shin—he groans in pain. He grabs a rock and throws it at me as I dive for his gun.

His men have stopped shooting at my friends, I can't see why. I hope they haven't been hit! Now they're aiming their guns at me!

I dive at Jono again, knowing that if I'm in close proximity with him, his men probably won't fire. I hope. We roll down the slope, tussling harder than I ever have before. I think we both know this is a fight to the death. We fall off a small ledge onto the river's eroded embankment. I land on top of him and don't hesitate to swing a mighty punch, which very clearly and audibly shatters his jaw. Blood pouring from his nose, he tries to kick me again. I just kick him in his side and tell him how rotten he is, in not so nice a word. All in one swift movement I reach down and pull his hand-gun from its holster, switch the safety off and point it at him. He looks up at me for a second and then laughs his evil laugh before becoming serious again. His voice is a lot more slurred this time from the injuries I've given him.

"You think you've beaten me? Look around you mate…"

I don't need to look up. He has four men with guns pointed at me, and another five pointing their guns at my friends, who thankfully are still alive.

"It was worth a try hey." I reluctantly place the gun on the ground and Jono picks it up.

The raging fire in his eyes has reached boiling point.

"Yeah… And now… You die."

Jason: A gunshot. Followed by another. And then several more until a full gun-fight erupts. I dive to the ground unsure of what is happening. Around me Jono's men are firing wildly into the bushland, falling one by one as they're hit by an unknown enemy. Jono is half-crouched, sheltered by the embankment. He glares as me as if to blame me for what is going on. I throw him a cheeky grin and shrug.

"Guardian angels?" I provoke Jono, and now he looks even more pissed off. I still can't see where the shooting is coming from. I assume Blake has something to do with it—he probably called the police.

Jono's men across the river have bolted after two of them fell to the ground wounded.

The firing stops.

I stand up slowly and look towards the dense scrub where the shooting was coming from. Eventually the lads emerge, Joseph leading the pack. All of them are there—Tooth, Mike, Jimmy and Benny. They're all armed to the teeth with weapons from our emergency stash. Handy idea in the end.

"Sorry we're late," Benny says. "Blake called us."

"Really?" I laugh, and wonder why he would call these guys.

"He said the police are on their way but you'll be dead by the time they get here. That's all the motivation we needed."

I shake my head, and can't believe I ever doubted these dudes. Or Blake.

I hear the sound of a gun cocking behind me.

The lads all swing their guns up towards Jono.

"Go ahead, shoot me. I don't care if I die." Jono stands up slowly, a maniacal look in his eyes, as I stare down the barrel of his gun. He ignores the continuous warnings from my mates to put his weapon down. "I don't even know why I allowed things to get this far, but that's just the way it goes sometimes. You were always a good ally Jason. You were always there to back up my crew and you always had the best goods. But you've been an even more worthy enemy. I'm sorry it has to end like this..."

"It doesn't have to end like this Jono," I plead with him, also signalling to my lads not to shoot. "Just put the gun down and we can all go home to fight again another day." I step closer, palms out in an attempt to offer peace. "I'm sorry about Paul..."

"Too late for apologies," Jono says and pulls the trigger.

I feel the pain instantly as the bullet enters my abdomen and I fall slowly to the ground clutching the puncture wound to stop the blood from spilling out. The world around me seems to go in slow motion and I feel detached from my body. I can hear more gunshots but can't see where from. I hear the sound of a helicopter, or maybe I'm imagining it.

I feel myself fading away and can barely focus enough to recognise all my friends who are now by my side. I close my eyes and think about Kate and Kelly. I picture the moment when Kelly was born and I held her for the first time. I remember thinking on that day I have something to live for again. I still cannot believe I helped create something so beautiful. I picture my family and remember all the amazing times we had together. I am sad that it looks like I will be leaving this place and Kelly won't know her real father. But my heart has been desperately aching for my family for so long.

Finally I will be with them again.

Chapter 17

~ *C'est La Vie* ~

Blake Solomon stands in shock in the emergency room watching doctors and nurses attempt to resuscitate Jason's lifeless body.

"How did it come to this?" He mumbles the question to himself in disbelief.

One of the doctors rushes over to Blake.

"Sir, we've been doing surgery for a few hours now but his pulse is still fading. We believe that any further attempts at resuscitation will be unsuccessful, what would you like us to do?"

Blake stares blankly at the doctor and then at the motionless boy lying on the gurney. He had done everything in his power to save him, this kid. He remembers being in this hospital not too long ago, but for a very different reason—to find these four amazing young people with him in this room. He just wishes it was himself in the place of Jason. He feels guilty that he didn't do enough to protect him.

Blake looks at the other three and they all shake their heads.

"Don't stop," Rebecca whimpers. "Please."

"He has lost a lot of blood," the doctor continues. "We will continue because he is young, and at your wishes, but don't get your hopes up." A nurse beckons to the doctor so he rushes back in to assist with the resuscitation.

Felicity and Rebecca both burst out into tears. A nurse rushes over to them.

"Maybe it's best that you go out to the waiting room. We'll keep you informed as to what's happening."

Blake leads the way and the four of them sit anxiously, holding each other close. For the first time, they sit in silence, no selfish thoughts entering their minds, nervously awaiting the news about their companion.

After what feels like hours, the same doctor strolls out of the operating room looking quite flustered. He walks over to the four, looking uneasy. Felicity and Rebecca have terrified expressions, Matthew looks more anxious than ever and Blake just looks bewildered.

"He's going to make it," the doctor finally spits out. "We fixed the bullet wound which had nicked a major vessel. His spinal cord was also damaged, so he may never walk again. He'll be kept under intensive care now until he is well enough. We'll let you in to see him when he wakes up."

Rebecca: "Oh my God! Thank you!" I scream and jump up and down and give the others the tightest hugs ever. This is the best news I've ever heard, I cannot believe it! It's a miracle. All my progress would've just gone straight out the window if Jason died. He may be a rough, arrogant thug, but deep down he has the same heart and soul as us all. We can all assume, or hope that he will quit the thug-life for good now—a person can only be shot so many times before they make the sensible choice!

"What's going to happen now?" Matthew asks Blake.

"Hmmm," Blake says thoughtfully, his face showing a new glow. "First we'll spend some time with Jason, and then head back to the ranch for the party."

We had been helping the staff of the clinic prepare for a beach party before all this happened. It's such a shame Jason won't be able to join us but it gives us an excuse to throw another party for him!

"I just wanna go home," Felicity moans. She looks up and notices mine and Matt's glares. "Oops, sorry guys."

Awkward. I know she didn't mean it. She has been very sensitive about the fact that she has a home to go to after this.

We wait for another good two hours before a nurse comes out again to get us.

"You can see him now," she begins, hesitating. "He isn't waking up as soon as we'd hoped—we're suspecting he's received a brain injury from lack of oxygen. We don't know if he'll ever wake up, but you're still welcome to see him."

Felicity bursts out into tears, Matthew holds her close.

"Is he still able to hear us?" Blake asks.

"It's hard to say. It's possible. He's not responding to anything, but by all means still talk to him."

Our moment of glory has been shattered in the blink of an eye.

"Thanks for telling us."

We're all grateful for the hospital staff's honesty but we really wish they were lying this time. We walk sombrely into the ICU cubicle where Jason is lying, attached to dozens of different monitors and cords. Felicity walks straight over and grabs his hand, whispering something into his ear for a few moments. Matthew holds his other hand and just stares blankly, deep in thought.

I don't know what to say to Jason when it's my turn. I just hold his hand and have a sudden urge to do something that I have been avoiding the whole time in this program—something which I had intended never doing...

I will play my video for them all, right now. I look at Blake and gesture towards the television. He responds immediately and asks a nurse if it is possible. She smiles and takes the video to play it. The others realise what I am up to and position themselves for a good view. I step into the background, fearful of their reactions but terrified of my own. I just hope Jason is listening.

F**elicity:** Such a sad day. And now Rebecca is probably going to make it even more gloomy with her depressing video. I understand that she wants to show Jason as well, but it's not really an appropriate time I would've thought. Oh well, Blake doesn't seem to mind. I look up at the TV as the video starts playing.

The camera must be on the ground because all that is showing is Rebecca's legs and the edge of a cliff. I can hear her speaking but can't make out what she's saying. All of a sudden, Rebecca falls forward and disappears from view, as if she fell off the cliff! Immediately though, another person appears in view and reaches out, pulling Rebecca back just in time! I think we all gasped and then breathed a sigh of relief, even though we knew Rebecca was obviously safe. It was just unexpected that's all.

The camera goes black for a moment and then begins again with Rebecca sitting in front of a cave.

"...Hi guys, sorry about that, I hope I didn't scare ya! I just wanted to show you how serious I was about ending my life, right up until I became friends with you guys... I'll begin from as far back as I remember... Just promise me you won't cry or anything like that. I've done enough of that to last a lifetime.

I don't remember anything about my birth parents but I do remember living in a foster home when I was about six or seven. It could've been earlier but anyway...

My foster dad would beat me on a daily basis. I would come home from school and he would make me cook dinner, clean the house, and then he would give me a good beating. And that was when he was sober. Most nights he would get drunk, but I learnt quickly to find a good hiding spot by locking myself in the attic, where he could never get to me. I just had to put up with listening to the screams of my foster mum being beaten nearly to death.

On one particular day he was already drunk by the time I got home from school. And he had the chains ready for me. He chained me up in the basement, naked, and had his dirty, filthy way with me..." A single tear rolls down her face. "My foster mum, who I thought would've saved me, just stood there in the background watching and sniggering.

That happened countless times before I got the guts to run away. And by the time I did leave it was too late—the damage had already been done.

I stayed in a shelter for a while but it wasn't long before they organised another foster family. This family didn't sexually or physically abuse me but they looked down on me like I was worthless. The parents treated me like I was diseased and wouldn't even go near me and the kids called me terrible names. I put up with it for a while but couldn't handle the misery of being ignored. The things it did to my mind. So many horrible thoughts. One day I found my foster mum's valium pills and took a whole heap, hoping it would end all the pain. And it did. I didn't feel upset for days. I didn't feel anything for days.

That's how my drug dependency began.

My foster parents soon figured out that I had been stealing the pills and kicked me out—after a severe beating of course.

I went through the same process a couple more times—living on the streets, moving to a shelter, and then a foster home until I ran away or got kicked out. I figured I'd had enough when I was eleven or twelve and another one of my foster dads tried to have sex with me. He tried to convince me that it was okay because I wasn't his child. I actually kicked him pretty good in the nuts and ran out!

It wasn't long before Gustav Trig found me. I had just shot up in an alleyway with a few other junkies, loving the fact that a substance could take away all of my pain, when I felt myself being lifted up. I felt like I could see my body from above and it was being taken away. I screamed but nothing came out. I swung my fists and kicked wildly but my body stayed limp. Gus took me back to his place and there I slept it off. He actually gave me another couple of injections of something different when I stopped breathing—I never found out what it was. He saved my life."

I look back and see that Rebecca is crying, and realise that I am too.

"Naturally I felt I could trust this man who saved my life so I agreed to work for him, not knowing that I had practically just sold my soul. He gave me all the drugs I wanted, mainly pills of some sort, which helped to numb the pain and torment I was going through. He also gave me shelter—a tiny room with no window. There was a wardrobe filled with clothes that only an adult should wear—lingerie, leather, satin, skimpy costumes, you name it. Whatever the customer requested, I had to do it. I had to service Mr. Trig's customers ten to twenty times a day, six, sometimes seven days a week. At first it hurt like hell, not only physically, but also emotionally. After a while I didn't even notice it, I didn't even notice that I was there. I made sure I was on drugs most of the time, but I think taking those pills so often got me so resilient they wouldn't work very well. I'd beg Mr. Trig for some more, and something stronger. The times when I actually was sober, after I got through the withdrawals, I just tried to think of anything besides being reminded of that evil foster dad, where my pain began.

All I hope is that he hasn't gotten to any other kids.

I was allowed to go outside once every couple of days for a couple of hours. I wasn't allowed off the premises though. I remember one of the few times I managed to escape —I wandered through the markets and caught a tram to the beach, wading through the shallows, forgetting my worries for all but a moment. It was one of the happiest times I can recall. Until Gus' men caught up with me though. Apparently I was too young for this kind of work, but I was earning Gus far too much money for him to give me up. I had become famous in the underworld and disgusting lustful men came from far and wide to see what all the fuss was about. Sure enough though, the interest wore off as I got older and more screwed up by the drugs, but Gus kept coming in a few times a week to make sure I was still in top form. I always gave him my best, whatever that means."

Rebecca turns away, and looks like she's going to be sick—her face has gone a deathly white colour.

"It disgusts me even thinking about this, and I cannot believe I am actually finally telling someone. But I'm glad I have told you guys, and I trust you'll understand that I'm not proud of my life. I didn't ask to be treated like this. I wouldn't wish it upon my worst enemy! Being thrust into that life from such a young age, it was all I knew.

When I met Gus, I managed to block out any memories from before, so it felt like I hadn't done anything else in my life and knew nothing else—I barely even finished primary school. I didn't know how to feel about my life and struggled with a mixture of guilt, sadness, anger and frustration. I knew that something was wrong inside of me, something was missing. There was a deep, dark, haunting feeling that ate away at me every day. I knew it wasn't right, and I knew I couldn't escape unless I was dead.

So I tried to off myself.

I saved up lots of drugs, the syringes and pills that they gave me daily, and took as many as I could at once. I don't know how it didn't kill me but somehow I ended up here.

Being here has taught me many things. I have never been able to speak my mind, or feel wanted, nor had my own opinion or input valued. I wasn't used to getting the kind of attention you guys gave me. I was only ever used to the bad kind of attention, and that's all I felt I deserved. I felt kind of guilty when you guys were nice to me and an extremely dark feeling came over me and made me so depressed that I tried to jump off that cliff. Thankfully Jason was there to save me, which is amazing. I didn't think I deserved another chance to live a new and better life but now I know… Life is what it is. You've just got to take every chance life gives you and use it the best way you can. I just feel blessed that I've been given the gift of life and have been given a chance to start a new and better life…

Thank you Matthew, Jason, Felicity and Blake for being my first true friends and for showing me the life I have missed out on. I know it'll be a long, hard path of healing for me. So many years of pain and torment can't be forgotten overnight. But thanks for showing me that there is another way.

More importantly, thank you for showing me love.

You guys have made me feel loved for the first time."

A tear and smile. That says it all. Rebecca's smile matches the on-screen one and she looks genuinely happy and relieved for the first time. I think she is truly amazing to have been through all that stuff and come out so strong. We all walk over and surround her in a group hug.

We stand there in silence, Rebecca sobbing quietly. I close my eyes and feel refreshed and anew. I was wrong to ever doubt her.

"Rebecca." A quiet, gravelly voice interrupts our group hug. It is Jason, he has half-opened his eyes and is reaching out for Rebecca's hand. She takes it and he squeezes tight. "You are beautiful, you know that? Don't let anyone tell you otherwise okay?"

"Okay," Rebecca squeaks. Her bottom lip quivers as her wide grin appears again briefly before she returns to sobbing. "I'm so glad you're okay Jason. We were so worried!"

Jason just smiles and then lets out a big sigh before resting his eyes again.

"Thank you so much everyone, for everything," Rebecca says and hugs us all once more.

"That's ok. And thank you, Rebecca, for sharing that incredibly brave and courageous story with us," Blake says looking satisfied.

"Thanks Felicity," Rebecca whispers as she hugs me.

"Anytime," I reply genuinely.

We hug in our little group for a few more minutes and then everyone is suddenly really energetic and excited—talking and laughing, until the nurse tells us to quieten down. It's the first time I have seen the whole group this happy. It makes me smile, but I still feel sad that I haven't finished telling them my story. They probably won't want to hear it now after hearing Rebecca's! It doesn't matter, I probably shouldn't be telling these people anyway. I'm sure they'll think it's nothing compared to what they've been through anyway.

Visiting hours are over so we say our goodbyes to Jason. It looks like we'll be leaving him here to go back to the resort and hopefully he'll recover quickly. Blake mentioned something about group sessions with Jason once he's out of ICU and just in a ward. That'd be good! We jump into the awaiting mini-bus and although I am exhausted, my mind is racing at a million miles an hour and I am unable to rest on the trip back.

"Hey Felicity, you okay?" Matthew puts his arm around me and I smile back at him.

"Yeah, I'm okay thanks. Just thinking."

"About Rebecca's story?"

"Yeah, you could say that." I peer out the window as the scenery rushes by.

"I've finished off my video ya know," Matt continues. "Might show it later on, but not sure. You guys pretty much know the whole story now anyway. I just finished it for keepsakes."

"Cool! Yeah I'll have a look at it for you. I'd like that."

I stare past him and I know straight away that he can sense something is wrong even though I try to hide it.

"Felicity." He hugs me firmly. "Tell me what's on your mind."

I look up at him and half-smile. I need to tell him. I need to tell them all. It's eating away at me, this forced silence.

It will kill me.

"I can't."

Matthew: "It's okay sweetie," I say to her and hold her closer. I have no idea what it is she's not telling me but I don't mind anymore. She'll tell us when she's ready, or find another way to deal with whatever it is. I gently place her head in my lap so I can stroke her hair, hopefully soothing her into a much needed deep sleep. She must be extremely fatigued because it doesn't take long before she is snoring her pretty little head off! I chuckle and then decide to rest my eyes as well...

"We're home!" Blake calls out in delight as we drive through the front gates to the clinic. It is pitch black and must be well past mid-night by now so we all head straight to our beds and zonk out like never before.

After breakfast the next morning Blake gathers us in the main hall for a meeting.

"Now, as you all know, we are coming close to the end of this very successful and shall we say, exciting program. You have all been triumphant in your goals and have improved in leaps and bounds. I am proud of the courage you have all shown. I am amazed at what a strong-willed, determined, and compassionate bunch of people you are. However, after you leave here, you will go back to the world you left behind. There will be the temptation to take the easy, but dangerous road back to your old lives but that's just the easy way out. As I've mentioned before, when we make preparations for you to leave here, you'll still have sessions twice a week for the rest of the year. That way we'll keep in touch and make sure we're all doing okay.

You all have amazing potential, and I think you're smart enough to realise where you've gone wrong."

Gone wrong? What does he mean by that? I didn't ask to be born in a war-torn country, having to run away and lead the life of a vagrant. Gosh, sometimes Blake can be a bit annoying with his speeches, although I know he means well.

"In all of your cases it is because something very bad happened to you that none of you deserve. I want you to all know that. You deserve better.

So I put to you all a couple of options… You can leave here and go back to your lives, without thinking of the disastrous consequences. Or, you can leave here with the support of one another behind you to help you face your problems. Or you can face them on your own. It's up to you…

I will be coming with you next week on the bus home. You can be dropped wherever you like—obviously we've arranged safe housing for Bec and Matt so we'll drop you there. Furthermore I have organised for you all to be taken to special places where you can get your lives sorted—to face your demons."

Everyone looks a bit bewildered. Does that mean he has booked me a ticket back to my homeland? Or to where my family is? That's the only place I want to go. I highly doubt that. Even though the fighting is over, my family wouldn't have gone back there and I also doubt that Blake has been able to find out where they are.

Rebecca looks worried as well.

Suddenly she stands up as if to say something, stopping Blake in his tracks.

"So you're telling me you expect us to *face our demons*, as you call it, after only six or so weeks here? Do you honestly believe we'll be safe out there again? We've barely brushed off the cobwebs, and now that we're finally making some progress you're going to put us back where all our problems began?! What the hell are you thinking? What if I go overdose again and kill myself this time? You can't do this to me Blake! Not like this! Not now!"

Blake rushes over and pulls Rebecca in for a tight hug. She whimpers into his chest. The rest of us surround her and it turns into a group hug. Blake eventually pries back Bec's head, despite her efforts to keep her tears from us.

"Rebecca," Blake begins, his eyes also filling with tears. "I promise you this—I'm not going anywhere. I'll never leave you, especially when you need me most and I'm certainly not going to dump you back out there by yourself! We'll all be with you every step of the way. It'll be a long road of recovery but you've set out to a good start."

"I can't do it Blake," she sobs. "I'm just not strong enough. It's easy here because I'm surrounded by all the right people and things. But back there, I have nothing. I have no-one. I won't survive."

"Sweetie, remember when you first came here? You barely spoke a word. Now look at you—you've got the confidence to stand up and say how you feel with complete certainty. That shows an incredible strength of character and something you should be proud of. Keep going on this path and you will thrive. You will have struggles, no-one's denying it, but use this newfound strength and you'll get through any rough patch. And remember, you're not alone. We're with you all the way."

Rebecca glances around at the faces smiling back at her and a grin breaks through her pained expression. It looks like she wants to fight some more but is almost too exhausted and her shoulders slump again.

We've all had such an emotional roller-coaster the past few weeks. It's been incredibly challenging, especially having to deal with the racial taunts of Jason, but also having to face the truths in my life. Maybe when I get back to town I'll start applying for more jobs. One of our activities here was to write our own resume—mine didn't contain much work experience but I do have many skills that

I was able to put down. Living in a self-sufficient village back home, we all learnt many simple trades and handyman skills. I also learnt many skills I thought to be useless while homeless. I never really thought I could get a job with those skills but Blake seems to think so. At least if I got a job it'd keep me preoccupied from worrying about my family.

For the rest of the day we relax and help with the preparations for the beach party tonight. It is ideal weather for a beach party—blazing hot throughout the day so once the sun goes down it'll be perfect. Everyone looks chilled out and we haven't talked about anyone's problems or recent events all day. It's nice to have a rest from all that. Rebecca looks calmed and is doing a lot to help prepare tonight's food. I can't help but think that she is in the same boat as me. Tomorrow when Blake drops us home, where will he take us two? Felicity has a nice home to go to, but Rebecca and I have nowhere and no one. I know Blake has somewhere for us to stay for a while but it'll probably only be a short-term solution. I wonder if it has been playing on Rebecca's mind too. Surely Blake knows it concerns Bec going into other people's homes to stay. Hmmm we'll see.

"Okay everyone," Blake continues. "It's party time!"

Finally we are able to kick off our shoes and party! No alcohol of course, but Blake certainly has organised a smorgasbord of food and other surprises including a couple of dune-buggies for us to race around in. He has put up the dozens of photos he has taken over the past couple of months and they're cool.

"I'm too excited to sleep tonight!" Rebecca exclaims, running off and diving into the warm water. I don't think any of us will get any sleep tonight!

* * * *

"I love you sweetie," Anne wraps her arms around Blake. They stand on the beachfront watching the three youths carry on and have fun. "You've done a great job."

"Hmmm, thanks." Blake is thinking about something bothersome.

"Are you worried about Jason? He'll be okay."

"I know," Blake replies and sighs. "I'm thinking about the first group."

"Oh." Anne hugs him tighter.

Blake recalls the very first group of a similar program here at Anchor Beach. He knows what went wrong but still can't believe it went to hell so quickly.

Anne and Blake wander over to the site where one of the buildings was burnt down by the youths in the program.

Blake believes his first mistake was that the group was too large. They just split into ethnic groups and created huge tensions from day one.

By the end of the first week there had been several fights a day and each "gang" had taken over an area of the resort.

Blake has a coughing fit. Stress normally does this to him. He doesn't know why he lets this get to him still.

Blake decided after that first week to call more staff in to help. The people he hired weren't trained in this sort of treatment and actually made things worse. There was one guy, Bill, who undermined each and every one of the kids and made them feel worthless. For instance, there was one girl—Hannah, who was very similar to Rebecca. Bill would call her every name under the sun. Blake only found out afterwards that he actually tried to rape her.

Everything eventually reached boiling point after a lecture in the hall.

These kids hated being lectured to.

So they decided to unite with one another and go about destroying the place. They trashed every room they could find and set fire to the mess hall. Blake and Anne are standing on its ruins.

He remembers staring in disbelief at the mayhem.

Chairs and tables were thrown out of windows. All items of food in the kitchen found their way onto a wall or a ceiling or a staff-member.

The staff gave up trying to stop them and just left, only a few loyal to Blake and Anne remained.

The news crews arrived just after the police and fire department. It wasn't exactly the publicity Blake had hoped for. His life's work, his dream was going up in smoke in front of him.

Naturally, after this event, funding was dropped. He had to cancel the program and reassess what to do.

"Let it go," Anne whispers in Blake's ear. "Look at what you achieved with this group."

Blake nods and wipes away a tear.

"Nobody else would've given up their time and money for these lost children. Nobody else would even give them the time of day. But you came into their lives and gave them another path, one that they had long given up on. That is an amazing thing. I'm so proud of you for it."

Blake looks into his wife's gorgeous eyes and smiles. He is so happy to have been able to help these kids but sad for he knows it won't last. Not for him anyway. It can't. He's been too well for too long now. He was lucky to survive it the first time, but the evil life-sucking disease is back and Blake knows his time is running out.

"You should tell them," Anne says, reading Blake's mind.

"I will."

CHAPTER 18

~ *Never Look Back* ~

Felicity: Our last week here has been the best one yet. We're no longer discussing terrible things as much. We've been doing loads of confidence building activities and helping Blake prepare the place for the next group of kids. He's asked us to come back and help out whenever we can—I'd like that.

Last night I wrote Blake a letter. I will tell the others everything eventually, but I think Blake needs to know before we leave this place today. I read over the letter one last time before placing it on his desk:

> *"Dear Blake,*
> *Thank you for everything. I know it's your job to help us, but you're the first person I've met who actually genuinely cared about my problems and feelings. I feel sad to leave but excited at the life I can now begin. But before I leave I must tell you one more thing...*
> *I've told you about Ben dying of cancer, but I never actually told you the full story. He was diagnosed with liver cancer. Luckily the tumour had not spread to any other part of his body, yet, but it was too far along to be treated or removed. He needed a liver transplant. He went on a waiting list for a liver but the doctors*

said he would die before one became available unless they could find a live donor, someone who would give up a large part of their liver for him.

They told me it would grow back if I donated part of mine but I was scared. I couldn't believe I was the only person suitable to be a donor, and I couldn't handle all the pressure that my parents were giving me. They and the doctors said I could save his life, but I needed to act quickly.

I needed time to think.

I was already scared of hospitals after watching my brother go to them all his life and scared of what could happen if they stuffed it up. If they made an error I would die and Ben would live. I suppose that wouldn't have been all bad. Unless he died as well.

I still remember the day when I went to my parents after thinking about it all night to tell them that I would do it, that I would help my baby brother Ben.

It was too late.

He had died through the night, and I was left feeling guilty for his death.

My parents didn't speak to me for a long time and they still haven't mentioned anything about it since.

You're the first person I've told.

Thanks again Blake, for everything.

Love Felicity

Xoxo"

The bus driver sounds the horn to let us know he's arrived. As we walk outside there is a loud smashing noise and loads of swearing and yelling. We approach the bus as the next group of kids hop off. Two girls and two guys again. Why change a good combination? An emergency exit window from the bus is lying on the ground smashed. One of Blake's colleagues escorts them inside. As they walk past, one of the boys taunts us. I look at the others and they smile and shake their heads. The program goes on.

As the bus departs through the gates of the Anchor Beach Resort everybody on board stares in silence at this isolated, prison-turned-resort style compound where we all turned our lives around. I am sad to leave this place, where I made more progress in these short weeks than I did in the many years of seeing psychiatrists and counsellors. Blake was right when he said that amazing things can happen here. I am aware that there still is a lot more work to be done to keep my life on track, but I think I now have to tools and motivation to do so.

I think everyone has mixed feelings about leaving here, as well what is on the schedule for today. We've decided to be taken as a group to wherever we need to go to face our problems, together.

First on the list of course is to see Jason. Rebecca looks particularly excited about this fact, but at the same time seems pre-occupied with something else.

Blake walks down the aisle and passes me a package.

"Here are the belongings that were confiscated prior to joining the program," Blake explains before having one of his strange coughing fits. I never really noticed until now how often he actually does cough. Most of the time he seems to suppress the coughing until he has left the room. In this case he can't really step outside the moving bus so he pulls out his handkerchief, covers his mouth and heads back to the front. He must have a really bad cold or something.

I tip the contents of the package onto the seat next to me. Inside are my Versace sunglasses, a packet of cigarettes, some makeup and my beloved mobile phone. I pick up the phone and turn it on. Within a minute it registers the thirty-eight messages and forty missed calls that I have accrued over the past weeks. They are mostly from stalker boys or my fake girlfriends who have messaged because they want something, and not one to see how I am. I read a message from one of my so-called best friends Tatiana: *Flic, what's up with you? Why no call back? You better be comin to Jake's party tonight, bring your booze and limo. X.*

I screw my nose up in disgust, open up the window next to me and throw the phone out without a care in the world. I look through the back windscreen and watch it smash to smithereens, which brings a smile to my face. Matthew, who saw the whole thing smiles and joins me for a cuddle.

We arrive at the hospital a few hours later and find that Jason has been moved from the intensive care unit to a ward. He is recovering well and will be discharged in hopefully a week.

"So you're all going home now? Or thereabouts," Jason asks.

"Yep," I reply after waiting a moment for someone else to respond. Rebecca is by his side holding his hand.

"I'm going back to the brothel to face that scumbag," she says matter-of-factly. "I wish you could come."

Jason's eyes light up. He sits bolt-upright in his bed, wincing slightly in pain.

"I've been through more pain than this," he declares, and points to another scar in his side. "Get me that wheelchair."

"I'm not sure if they'll allow this mate." Blake looks concerned.

"Oh to hell with them," Jason says and pulls himself to sit on the edge of the bed. "You can bring me back later, but I'm not missing this for the world. And anyway Blake, you were able to break a wild bull like myself and set my life back on the right but long-lost road so why would you worry about what the people in this place think?"

"Yes you're right." Blake beckons to Matthew to grab the wheelchair and help Jason onto it. "I've just got to make a quick phone call before we leave."

Blake disappears for a little while as we wheel Jason down to the bus. Nobody even objects. They probably thought we were just taking him out for some fresh air. Matthew helps him up into the bus and then folds the wheelchair up so we can take it with us. Shortly, after Blake had returned we were on our way again.

First stop is my place. I have no idea what to expect. My parents know that I'm coming home but I wonder if they'll even bother waiting for me or off gallivanting.

When we arrive, I hesitate as I hop out of the bus. Matthew gives me a peck on the cheek for luck. He's so sweet! I walk up the steps to my front door, looking up at the huge townhouse, which I hate on sight but have grown to love because it has always been there for me no matter what. The others wait in the mini-bus, peering through the windows, eager to find out how I go. I try the front door, which is surprisingly unlocked, so I open it slowly and walk in.

"Mum? Dad?" I call out, not expecting an answer. There isn't.

I walk into the living room and my heart sinks. I see my mother in my dad's arms balling her eyes out.

"Oh my God, what's happened?" I say, fearing the worse.

My mother jumps up and rushes to give me a massive hug, the biggest one she has ever given me.

"Nothing dear," she reassures me between sobs. "We're just happy you're home."

My dad smiles at me widely, and I realise how much I want to tell them everything. There's something I must do first though. I break away from my mother's embrace and run upstairs. I find all of my little hiding spots and put every illicit substance, razor blade, condom, and alcohol in a big container and walk slowly back downstairs with it. I stare into the box at all the things that have kept me sane, or so I thought, for the past 3 or 4 years. Right now I feel as if I don't need any of it anymore, and I hope it stays this way. With my parents help and support I'm sure I'll be able to achieve this. I look my parents sincerely in the eyes before placing it on the coffee table in front of them.

"This has been me for the past few years." A warm tear rolls down my cheek. "Please don't hate me."

Both of my parents stare at the container for a brief moment before embracing me in a group hug.

"Felicity, we could never hate you," my dad reassures me. "We love you very much."

My moist eyes suddenly burst out into flowing tears, and we stand there crying and hugging, apologising, reassuring, and finally reunited as a family again.

Matthew: I stare through the window of Felicity's townhouse and watch them embrace each other until I can't look anymore. I'm excited and happy for her but I realise that the chances of that happening to me is slim to none. I guess I didn't try very hard in the past to locate my family, out of fear. I knew if they wanted to stay hidden they would. And I knew if they wanted to find me they would. Nevertheless I'm still keeping my hopes up! Blake seems to be capable of anything.

Eventually Felicity comes back out to the bus with a massive grin from ear to ear.

"Thanks guys!" She gives us all hugs, including Blake.

"No worries." Blake smiles. "Matthew, you're next. We've got a nice surprise for you downtown, so let's go!"

My heart is racing and I don't know what to say. I knew Blake had been phoning around to Government departments and refugee groups in search of my family but he hadn't given the slightest indication of whether he was successful or not. I hope it's not a false alarm! I don't want to get my hopes up for nothing.

We drive through town until we reach Macintyre Mall. Blake points me in the direction of a nice little café.

I take a few deep breaths, and the others give me words of encouragement, which I don't even register because I am so nervous and excited and anxious.

I enter the café and search the room for my parents. I cannot see them so I take a seat near the window in view of the bus. I guess my family is late, as usual!

Half an hour passes.

I am just about ready to give up and leave when I get a tap on the shoulder. I spin around, my mouth grinning widely to see two Caucasian men in suits.

"Are you Maliik Ngoudjo?" The stockily built man on the right says.

I nod but correct him—"Call me Matthew."

He reaches out his hand for me to shake followed by the second man. This isn't exactly what I had in mind when Blake mentioned a surprise.

"My name's William Johnson, and I'm from the immigration department, and this here is Richard Sercombe. May we take a seat?"

"Oh," I say surprised. "Yes of course."

They sit in front of me, neither of them smiling, which alone makes my stomach churn wildly.

"I have some good news and some bad news I'm afraid," William Johnson begins. "The bad news is that we have been unable to locate your family, as they are obviously playing it safe and have most likely changed their names to keep us from deporting them. Part of the good news is that we do not want to deport them at all. They will just have to go through the correct process of migration. That is of course if we can find them. We believe you can help us with this…"

"And that's where I come in," Richard Sercombe interrupts. "William here didn't introduce me properly. I am actually from Beanpole Productions, and we would like to purchase the rights for the film you made while at the rehabilitation clinic. We are currently under contract with a Government campaign which is for the plight of refugees running from the Central African War, which I understand is where you came from."

William takes his turn to interrupt. "Many thousands of innocent people from your country illegally immigrated to our shores under the fear of not only the fighting and genocide in your homeland but also the oppression of strict local Government policies. These policies have since been changed due to the severity of the war and how it has impacted upon the global community, and we are aiming to do whatever we can to help…"

"So this campaign will share your story with Australians, as well as hopefully spreading the message to those who are seeking asylum here that they will be looked after and not be treated like prisoners, or worse still, deported."

"By having your story out there, it will also help us find your family."

Jason: Good luck to him, Matthew. I don't know what they're talking about but by the look on Matthew's gleaming face right now as he stands and shakes the men's hands I can bet that it's something good.

Matthew jumps back onto the bus, beaming like I've never seen before. He explains what happened and thanks everyone for supporting him, especially Blake. I give him a good pat on the back and a smile—the first genuine one I've ever given a black person since my family were killed. I don't know if Blake purposely put Matthew and I in the same group for a reason, but there's one thing I know for certain now—Matthew saved my life. Literally, and by helping me escape from the deadly downwards spiral I was being thrust into with no escape. I can now honestly and truly say from my heart that I no longer hate black people. Maybe I never even actually did hate them. Perhaps I just hated the people who killed my family, and it didn't matter what colour their skin was, but I just needed an excuse to hate something or someone in order for me to seek revenge and an outlet for my anger and resentment. I took the easy, but deadly one-way road of loathing and anger. Whatever the reason, I no longer have those feelings anymore, and I know that I can actually start feeling happy and enjoy my life. I will never understand why my family was taken from me, and why I was left behind to suffer, but I now know that there are a lot of things that cannot be explained but we just have to take what we're given as it comes and deal with it, no matter how difficult or challenging it may be.

We drive through the suburbs until we reach my neighbourhood, and I start to get butterflies. Blake mentioned organising something for me before we left the hospital. But I don't really want to go straight back home. I don't want to go back to my apartment, where anyone could be waiting to attack me. Wow, that's a first—avoiding confrontation. I do wanna see the boys though, to thank them, and explain my situation. I take a deep breath and prepare myself for the worse as we round my street corner. However, the bus doesn't slow down as we pass my apartment block.

"Hey!" I call out to the bus driver. "My place is back there!"

"It's okay Jason," Blake reassures me. "We're not going there. Trust me."

I am very relieved but try not to show it. I wonder where the hell we are going then? We continue driving for several more kilometres, passing Kate's house, which has a sold sign out the front. I hang my head, realising where we are going. I knew the police had spoken to Blake and they had come to an agreement that I could stay at the rehab clinic as long as I turned myself in for questioning upon arrival back into town. I guess Blake is strong to his word, so I cannot blame him for doing the right thing. I just wanted to be there for Rebecca when she went to face her boss.

I wave goodbye to the others as Blake wheels me into the police station.

"I'm sorry I have to do this Jason," Blake apologises on the way in. "I have to abide by the law though."

"That's okay, I understand."

The officer at the front desk recognises me straight away and takes me into a private room where the sergeant in charge speaks to me.

"Hi Jason, it's good to see you again. Now, since your little rumble we've actually had the quietest week in years! It seems that everyone is in hiding after that. I'll get straight to the point so you can sort your other stuff out. I'm going to offer you a deal. All you need to do is testify against Jono and a few other members of his gang and we can sign this release form to clear you of all charges that were going to be pressed against you. This doesn't happen very often, but these are special circumstances, and we have been informed of your situation by Dr. Solomon."

That's the first time I've heard anyone call him "Doctor". I sign the form without hesitation and I'm sent off with no further questions.

"That didn't take long." Blake smiles cheekily as he wheels me back to the bus.

"Yeah… I don't know what to say Blake, but thank you!"

"That was nothing… We're not finished yet!"

Oh my God, my heart races as the bus takes off and I have a good feeling about where we're heading—to see Kate and Kelly!

I don't think I'll ever be able to wipe this wide grin off of my face! I stand corrected, and frown when I realise where we are going. The bus drives for another half an hour and makes the turn into Centennial Park—the town's biggest cemetery. The cemetery where my family is buried. I look at Blake as he helps me out of the bus.

"How did you know where to find them?"

Blake shrugs again and brushes off yet another mystery.

He wheels me to the large burial plot where my family lie side-by-side. I haven't been here since the funeral—I've tried to avoid it all these years out of fear of completely losing myself. I'd chosen a completely different life to the one my parents had laid out for me, in order to have minimal reminders of these wonderful people. Blake leaves me sitting there, a big sorry sack, in front of the Parker family plot, crying my eyes out genuinely for the first time since that fateful night. I search my pockets for something to wipe my nose with but come up empty.

A hand immediately presents itself in front of me with a female's handkerchief. I recognise it as one of Kate's.

I swing around to see her holding Kelly, the two of them dressed in black. Kate and I met after my family had passed away and I never really told her much about it. I guess now is as good a time as any.

I cradle Kelly, admiring her lovingly. Kate kisses me on the cheek and wraps her petite arms around my shoulders.

"I love you both," I say to them. "And I'm never letting you go."

R**ebecca:** Oh God, oh man, oh bloody hell! I haven't been able to concentrate this entire trip! As soon as Jason's visit was over I knew there was no turning back now for me. I hope I've seemed happy for the others but all I can think about is going back to that horrible place and seeing all the girls again and the vile customers and of course, Mr. Trig. I think I'm about to hyperventilate, my chest is becoming tighter, my palms are becoming sweaty and my stomach is doing somersaults. I don't want to go in there by myself, let alone at all!

It takes another hour to get there but when we pull up out the front I burst out into tears.

"I can't do this!" I grab Jason and sob into his sleeve.

"It's okay Rebecca," Blake tries to comfort me. "We can do this together."

I look up at Blake who is gazing at me sincerely and lovingly.

"Really?"

"Absolutely."

There are also a dozen police officers and welfare workers here to assist in shutting down this place. They're going to give me a chance to face Gus first though. Apparently they've tried a few times to catch him but he's very sneaky. Sometimes he even has someone else sit in his office pretending they're Gus in case the cops come.

I take several deep breaths before walking up to the gate and pressing the buzzer.

"*…Hello, who is this?*"

I instantly recognise Gus' voice over the intercom, which makes me feel even sicker in the stomach.

"Um… It's Rebecca."

"*…My angel? Come in my sweetheart!*"

God I hate it how he calls me that—*angel*. The gate swings open, so I walk up to the huge front doors, followed by Blake. The police sneak in and hide on either side of the door. The windows have roller shutters, which are always down, to hide the illegal activities that go on in this horrible place. The door swings open and we walk in, guided by one of the senior girls, Lana.

"Who the hell is this?" She says, glaring at Blake.

"He's um…"

Oh crap, what do I say. I can't let her know who Blake really is or they'll hurt both of us and they'll try to lock me in this prison forever.

"I'm a customer of hers," Blake says bluntly.

Lana looks him up and down and smiles.

"Good, I'll let Gus know. He's waiting for you in his office."

I nod and fake a smile. I remember hearing stories from the other girls about how Gus had a brothel in another city and some undercover police officers came to arrest him. However one of the girls, it could've been Lana, suspected something and alerted Gus who managed to escape. Stupid snitch. I guess they've still got the same suspicions of whoever enters this building. And that's why the cops hid when she opened the door, otherwise she probably would've locked us out.

After climbing two flights of stairs we reach Gus' office. He's left the door open so I enter, with Blake waiting just outside so he can hear if I need him.

"Rebecca, my darling!" Gus, the disgusting, vile creature gives me a kiss on both cheeks, choking me with the smell of booze and tobacco. "It's great to see that you're well, and even better that you came back to me! But, unfortunately, you've seen what happens to the naughty girls..."

The very sight of his thin, black moustache, and pock-marked face makes me even sicker, but with rage this time. This stout, balding, pathetic little man has controlled my life for far too long and it is going to end right here, right now, whether he likes it or not.

"I hate you Gus." I spit at him. "You have used and abused me for too long and it ends now. I hate the way you preyed on me when I was weak and vulnerable, and needed someone to protect me. I wasn't even a teenager and you still took away my only shred of dignity and innocence and destroyed it with drugs and prostitution. I was only a child! You took away my life, and made it worthless, driving me to suicide. I would've done anything to get away from you but you wouldn't let me, as if you owned me. I'm glad I didn't die because I can't wait to see your pathetic little face whimpering when they lock you up."

Gus takes a long drag on his cigar. The smoke looks blurry through my teary eyes.

"Now, now, now, Rebecca, let's not get nasty. Don't forget who saved your life in the first place—numerous times actually. I gave you a life—one which you enjoyed so much that you're back here now, knowing full well that I won't let you go this time. There's no escape my darling. Not this time. And we won't be supplying you with drugs anymore because we don't want you trying to end your useless, pathetic little life while you can still please my customers, and me... So let me see if you still have it sweetheart..."

He wanders over to me, looking at me suggestively. Yeah, you just try anything buddy and it'll be the end of your manhood, believe me. He strolls over to close the door but is stopped by Blake's bulging arm.

"What the... Who the hell are you?"

"It seems I'm being asked that a lot today... I'm Blake Solomon, and your time is up."

I pull out the sound recorder, which I had in my jacket pocket.

"We recorded the whole conversation, which we probably won't even need because the evidence is all here, in this building."

Gus lets out one of his evil little laughs, which stops abruptly when he becomes serious. What a loser.

"You think you've won do you? You have no idea. I've prepared for every eventuality, including this one. Why do you think I have this?" Gus pulls out a pistol and points it at Blake. "I have men downstairs ready to take you away and make you disappear forever. I'll erase the both of you if I have to, as if you never existed. Then, if you just happened to have told the cops my location, I have escape tunnels leading to... well I'm not going to tell you that, but just know that I can escape any situation. And I have earned enough money from little sluts like you to last me a dozen lifetimes."

God, he makes me so angry. He's the one with no idea! He will rot in jail and I will be glad to see him sent there.

"Don't you dare point that at him," I say calmly to Gus while stepping in front of the gun.

"Oh, so that's the way it is, is it? Well that doesn't bother me. I've got plenty of girls where you came from. And they're loyal to me, unlike yourself."

The snarl in Gus' voice makes me realise that he is serious about killing us both, and I begin to panic. I've only ever heard his voice like this when he was so angry with one of the girls that he almost beat her to death.

"Put the gun away chump," Matthew says as he walks swiftly over to him. Gus doesn't know who to point the gun at. Instead he points it at himself. Matthew pushes the gun away just as it fires, creating a hole in the ceiling and a shower of plaster over us. Matthew and Blake wrench the gun away from him and tackle him to the floor. Matthew puts his knee into Gus' neck so that he is unable to move. I run over and hug them both.

"Thank you guys! I was beginning to wonder where you were Matthew!"

"You won't get away with this!" Gus tries to shout but is muffled by the weight of Matthew on him. "My bodyguards will be here to kill you all in a matter of seconds."

How pathetic.

"No they won't actually," Matthew begins. "I had some help from a man in a wheelchair and we, um, sorted them out."

I smile with joy. I'm sure Jason would've loved to have been able to get up the stairs to see all this.

I can hear some of the girls screaming and there is a lot of commotion downstairs.

"What the hell?" Gus looks confused.

"Oh yeah, I forgot to mention. We brought the police with us." I give him a hard kick in the nuts for good measure.

The police enter moments later and arrest the sorry little man and as he is marched down the stairway everyone in the whole building goes silent. One of the girls yells out—"Go to hell asshole!" Everyone cheers. All of the girls Gustav Trig once imprisoned in this place are now free.

And so am I.

On our way home we stop at Felicity's house to have dinner and end up chatting all night long because we are all brimming with excitement after today's events. Blake makes mention that the State Government has granted funding for the Anchor Beach Resort to continue the Another Chance at Life program. The location is still going to be protected though, to avoid extreme circumstances like what happened with us! Blake also explained where Matt and I will be situated until more permanent housing becomes available. We'll be staying with him and Anne! Blake reckons I'm still very fragile and will be for a while so he wants to make sure I'm looked after. He's right—I do feel fragile, like at any point if I don't get the support he's promised I'll fall again. But it's a starting point for a new life and I'm excited about that and willing to do whatever it takes. There will be tough times ahead, for a long time I'm sure, but at least I'm not alone anymore.

When it's time to leave Felicity's there are a few tears and I feel sad again. I'm glad we're catching up in town a couple of times a week as a group, because I'm gonna miss these guys so much.

I may not have been able to find my real family, not yet anyway, but I have made life-long friends in these people here. They're my best friends. They *are* my family.

EPILOGUE

~ *That's Life* ~

Felicity: Here we are, all together here in this place again. We got news of the location and reason for this gathering a few days ago and once again I am left not knowing how to feel. It's been six months since we've all been here together and I have mixed feelings. Nobody has spoken, but just smiled in acknowledgement and respect as we stand in a circle on Anchor Beach, the very place where we first met. The sun is setting, the air is fresh, and there is the peaceful sound of waves crashing onto the shore. Blake loved this place, and it feels like the right thing to do, to be here for this occasion.

Blake's wife Anne stands at the head of his coffin to say a few words.

"This is exactly how Blake wanted his funeral; in such a beautiful location, surrounded by the people he loved and cherished the most in this world. Let me tell you a few things about my husband. Blake had many aspirations in life. After our son Jacob was killed in a car accident, only days after getting his licence, Blake put his life on hold and disappeared into the wilderness for six-months to find himself. Once he returned he decided to travel the world and help those less fortunate than him with education, shelter, food, and medical assistance. He was so sad to see how selfish the world was becoming, and often felt that his contribution was insignificant. This never discouraged him though, and he always put other people before himself and never asked for anything in return. Everyone he met he cared about, no matter what their background, history or culture. I knew how much he loved me, but often I felt that he cared more about the children who were suffering, and this is a trait that I love dearly in Blake. Not long after returning from many years overseas, Blake became seriously ill with cancer."

As tears stream down my face, I refuse to look at the others because I know that if I see any one of them crying I will lose myself. My head is throbbing and I feel like my face is burning up and about to explode. My lips are quivering as I stare at the coffin, which is covered in colourful flowers.

"He battled cancer for many years and while bed-stricken he became passionate about something that was occurring closer to home. He began to notice, while spending so much time in hospitals, the amount of troubled young people that came and went and he got his heart set on helping them. Most of these kids didn't want help and would often run away again and get into even more trouble. But he never gave up. The doctors said it was a miracle that he survived his fight with cancer for this long, but I believe God needed him on Earth for a while longer. He closed his town clinic to set up the rehabilitation clinic here on this beach. He chose this location because of its remoteness, its beauty and its relevance. An old mental institution, it had been abandoned for many years so Blake did the place up to make it suitable for the younger generations and organised a program called Another Chance at Life. And so he began, reaching out to those in desperate need of help and loving them unconditionally until they realised they deserved another chance. He gave them the opportunity to face their demons."

This time I do look up. I look at the faces of my friends. We are all holding each other's hands now and smiling weakly, with reddened, blood-shot eyes from crying. We only knew Blake for a few months, but he touched our hearts with his generosity, unconditional loving-kindness, and I think most of all, his faith in us.

Rebecca looks really healthy now, and from what I've heard she is doing well. She has been staying with Anne still, and Blake til he passed away. She's enjoying helping with the new groups, we've all helped out a few times, and shown our videos. Bec is also studying to get her high school equivalency, which I think is pretty cool. Straight A's so far from what I've heard!

Matthew is also doing very well. His video was an instant hit, causing a world-wide stir—you could even say an uproar in protests against the criminals who tried to overrun his country. It even helped stimulate the Government's decision to provide more aid to countries in need. These countries are finally getting the media coverage they need. The video was also seen by Matthew's family who immediately sought him out. His father told me how proud he is of him, and that they had tried many times to find him. It was actually Matthew who had stayed off the radar! One thing that upset me a bit was that they disagreed when Matt mentioned his feelings for me. We talked about it and agreed to just be friends. For now. His family are fit and well. They are standing beside him right now.

Jason reunited completely with his family, well I mean, the family he has made—Kate and Kelly. He popped the question so they're getting married next year. Jason reunited with his mate Dave who will be his best man at the wedding, and is standing with them today as support. Jason is finishing his law degree—he says that rather than defending crooks, he wants to help people such as himself caught in bad situations. Many things have changed in our hometown recently. Ever since he testified against Jono, which was highly publicised, keeping Jason anonymous of course, the ganglands of this town seem to have dissolved. The police have had the quietest six months ever.

As for me, I am happy at last. My parents have finally told me they forgive me, even though they swear they never blamed me for Ben's death. They said that they were just grieving in their own ways and finding it hard to understand why he had to die so young. My dad was never running off with other women, besides the one time I caught him—he was actually going to rehab himself for alcoholism, which started after the death. Mum and dad have talked through their issues and sought counselling so we're on the right track again. I love my new group of friends. I'm not too proud of the reasons why we met but I guess everything happens in life for a purpose. I still don't know how I wasn't killed when I cut myself that fateful afternoon, and I don't know how my friends here survived either. Maybe it was luck, maybe it was the skills of the paramedics, nurses and doctors who worked on us, or maybe it was some higher force that I, and no-one will ever completely know or understand. Whatever it was, I'm glad I got another chance. We are all still scarred in different ways, physically and emotionally, but we have won the battles and challenges we were faced with. We will never forget what Blake did for us. We will never forget Blake.

After singing 'Amazing Grace', Blake's wife concludes with one last, short but powerful sentence that causes a shiver to go up my spine.

I step forward and place my flower onto Blake Solomon's coffin and walk away, without looking back. His grave will forever be here in this place, and he will forever be in my heart. I repeat Anne's final sentence in my mind, as I also put to rest any more pain and anguish that has been heavy on my heart.

"Blake was given a second chance to make something of his life and he passed it on to those who thought they did not deserve such grace."

ACKNOWLEDGEMENTS

Although this section may not mean much to most readers, you should all know that without *you* my stories wouldn't be heard, so thank you for reading.

The people I mention here have assisted me in their own different ways and nothing has gone unnoticed or unappreciated.

I would like to thank my amazing friends and family who have supported me through every journey I have chosen to take in life. You know who you are. Thanks to those of you who read through my work and gave me valuable insight or words of encouragement.

Special mentions must go to my parents for fear of leaving anyone out. Geoff and Charisse—thanks for believing in me and always being there to support me. To my brothers Ben and Jono, cheers for your brotherly kind words, and for letting me use your names in my work. There are too many friends who've helped in different ways so I dare not mention you all for fear of leaving anyone out. To my beautiful partner Brianna—I cannot even begin to describe how much I appreciate and love your constant support and unconditional faith in me. To my close friends Dave Simpson and Benny Dowie. Thanks Dave for hassling me to let you read the book well before I'd even finished the first chapter. Thanks Benny for designing the awesome cover.

Thank you to the assessors of Driftwood Manuscripts for giving me your insight and pearls of wisdom that helped this novel to reach its full potential.

Once again, thank you *all* for reading.

About the Author

Ashley Sanders was born in Adelaide, South Australia in 1984, where he has lived most of his life. He attended Eynesbury College before completely a Bachelor of Health Sciences at Flinders University. He then went on to become a Paramedic with the SA Ambulance Service.

Ashley found his love for writing throughout school and University, and has finished half a dozen manuscripts. Facing Demons is the first novel he has had published so far, and he plans to produce many more. He is currently working on Prequels to Facing Demons, which explore the lives of the main characters prior to meeting one another. He has also written several screenplays, one of which is being produced into a mini-series.

Contact the Author

Ashley can be contacted via email at: ashleysanders@live.com.au
Or follow him on facebook or twitter.
Blog: bazzavswild.blogspot.com